DESIRE FOR THREE

Desire, Oklahoma 1

D0841646

Leah Brooke

EROTIC ROMANCE

Siren Publishing, Inc.
www.SirenPublishing.com

A SIREN PUBLISHING BOOK
IMPRINT: Erotic Romance

DESIRE FOR THREE
Desire, Oklahoma 1
Copyright © 2008 by Leah Brooke

ISBN-10: 1-60601-239-8
ISBN-13: 978-1-60601-239-0

First Publication: November 2008

Cover design by Jinger Heaston
All cover art and logo copyright © 2008 by Siren Publishing, Inc.

PUBLISHER
Siren Publishing, Inc.
www.SirenPublishing.com

DESIRE FOR THREE
Desire, Oklahoma 1

Leah Brooke
Copyright © 2008

Chapter 1

Clay Erickson glanced at his brother, Rio Erickson, before returning his attention to the three Preston brothers.

"Full house!" Ben Preston laughed as he fanned his cards on the table. "Kings full of fives!"

Clay grimaced as he threw down his three aces. "Looks like you're on a winning streak tonight, Ben."

"On a winning streak here." Wade Preston chuckled. "At home, he's in the doghouse with Isabel," he referred to their wife and the third Preston brother, Cord, snickered in response. "Cord and I have been trying to get Isabel to forgive him, but so far she hasn't."

Ben glared at his two brothers. "I don't care how pissed she is. She deserved a spanking and she got it!" He downed his whiskey with a grimace.

"She enjoyed that spanking, too, which only pissed her off even more." Wade shook his head. "I wish I had gotten to her first. She knows to check that she has her cell phone with her. Anything could have happened to her on the trip to Tulsa."

"You're preaching to the choir," Cord said as he dealt the next hand. "I told her that if I had gotten to her first, it would have been my hand making her ass burn. Her mad won't last long. She knows we're only trying to take care of her just like we always have."

Wade placed his bet. "We'll go home early tonight and end this." He smiled in anticipation.

Clay and Rio absorbed the conversation between the Preston brothers. Ben, Wade, and Cord Prestons had married Isabel more than thirty years ago and had three grown sons. No one could doubt the love these men had for their wife. It showed clearly on their faces and you could hear it in their voices whenever they talked about her.

Several men had gathered at the club, some playing poker, others just talking, everyone with one eye on the activity taking place on the other side of the large room.

Two club members, Brandon Weston and Ethan Sullivan, had a naked woman—a new sub—between them. "Fuck me, damn you!" she screamed.

Both men laughed as she sobbed her arousal. Ethan's hand landed hard on her ass as she lay bent over a table. Both men were also naked, their cocks hard and throbbing as they aroused the woman. Her nipples were hard and red, her thighs wet as her juices flowed from her pussy.

Brandon held the back of her head in one hand and he stroked his cock with the other as he slowly pushed past her open lips.

"Come on, honey, open wider," he urged as he began a smooth rhythm of strokes into her waiting mouth almost carefully as if not to push too far.

Groans could be heard around the room as Ethan used the woman's own juices to prepare her anus for his cock. Running his fingers through her juices and into her anus, he stroked her and she whimpered with pleasure.

She sucked Brandon even harder, demanding in her arousal. When Ethan added another finger, she moaned, pushing back against his hand to force his fingers deeper. He gave her what she wanted, stretching her to take him.

"Hurry up, Ethan," Brandon growled. The strain of holding back hardened his features. "She's wicked with her mouth."

Ethan slowly drew his fingers from her tight ass, chuckling as she strained to follow. Holding her in place with a strong hand on her hip, he wrapped a hand around his straining cock, poising the head at her tight entrance. The excitement level in the room rose as he slowly pushed past the tight ring of muscle. The woman bucked as the head of his cock disappeared inside her.

"Easy, sweetheart," Brandon crooned to her as he plucked and tugged at her beaded nipples, reddened from their previous ministrations. "You'll have all of it. Just relax so Ethan can shove his cock all the way up that beautiful ass."

Over her back, he watched as his friend moved, his strokes deeper and deeper, wringing continuous moans from her. Brandon pulled his cock from her mouth as Ethan wrapped an arm around her waist, pulling her back against his chest. Brandon moved to lie at the end of the table and Ethan brought the wriggling woman closer.

She looked beautiful, flushed with arousal, arching in Ethan's arms trying to reach fulfillment. But Ethan held her tightly against his chest, not giving her room to move as Brandon got into position beneath her, positioning himself at the entrance to her pussy. Slowly Ethan lowered her onto his friend's throbbing erection.

"Fuck me!" she screamed when both men were finally seated to the hilt inside her. The men groaned at the tightness as they quickly established a well practiced rhythm. As she screamed out her release, the two men continued to fuck her, pounding into her now as a second orgasm gripped her. Both men cried out as they came, drenched in sweat, holding the now exhausted woman tightly between them.

Clay pulled his gaze away from the training session to look at his brother before he turned back to the game. "Brandon and Ethan seem to be enjoying themselves."

Rio nodded. "They usually do. Having everyone stay at their hotel works out for them. They make the money for the rooms and they meet all the new subs recruited. This one must be a new one. I don't recognize her."

Club Desire hosted training sessions for Doms twice a year. The wannabe Doms stayed at Brandon and Ethan's hotel next door. Women who lived the lifestyle full time but had no permanent Dom and women who only dabbled in it came to Desire, Oklahoma to participate. Some came year after year, using their vacation time from their jobs to join in the training, fulfilling their fantasies before returning back to the real world. Others came hoping to find a Dom who would keep them.

They included attorneys, doctors and accountants, along with waitresses, and even a school teacher.

Most of the club's members lived in the town of Desire, where they met to discuss and compare notes on the lifestyle they had chosen to lead. The club members gave each other advice and support, always exploring new ways to give pleasure to the women in their lives. No one criticized another's lifestyle as long as it was consensual and no one got hurt.

Rio watched as Brandon lifted the woman in his arms and carried her from the room, his buddy Ethan walking beside them, rubbing her back. As they left the room, he turned to Cord Preston. "I gotta ask you this. Why in the world would you tell Isabel that you would have been the one to spank her if you had gotten to her first?" He shook his head in confusion. "She wasn't pissed at you, just Ben. Didn't that make her mad at you, too?"

Cord laughed as his two brothers chuckled. "Oh, yeah, it did. But, if you boys are gonna share a woman, you'd better learn to stick together."

Ben leaned forward, his eyes full of pity as he regarded Clay and Rio. "You were so young when your parents died, too young to really understand your parents' relationship. We would have explained how everything worked in this kind of relationship, but when you got married to two different women, we didn't see the point."

Wade jumped in. "Even though there are three of us, Isabel rules the house. Believe me, when she's not happy, *nobody's* happy. We rule in the bedroom only because she allows it. No still means no, but if you learn how to love your woman, you'll never hear that word. But you are still the man of the house and have a responsibility to take care of your woman, to do what is best for her. She may not always agree with what you think is best, which is when you have to put your foot down."

"Which is what happened with us," Cord told them. "Isabel knows that she is always supposed to have her cell phone on her and that it should be on. We want to be able to check on her and make sure she's alright and we want her to be able to call one of us when she has a problem. But she forgot to take it with her when she went to Tulsa with a friend for the day." He shrugged. "It was an honest mistake, one any of us could have made, but by spanking her ass red, hopefully she'll think about it the next time she goes out and not forget it again."

Ben banged his fist on the table. "If spanking her bottom means that she'll have her phone with her when she needs us, I would do it a hundred more times. We don't do anything that isn't in her own best interest." He regarded Clay and Rio. "It will be up to the two of you to decide what is best for your woman, but you have to agree on it or it will never work. If she can divide you on your thinking, she can end up not respecting either one of you because you don't stand up to her. A woman needs to know that her men are strong enough to handle her."

Clay sighed. "What happens if we get it wrong?" He eyed the three brothers. "I remember how much love and laughter there was in our house when we were growing up. I see how much all of you love Isabel."

"That we do," Ben agreed.

"Without a doubt," Wade replied readily.

"More than life," Cord added.

"See, that's what I mean. And everyone knows how much Isabel loves the three of you. We want what the three of you have, a woman who you all love and that loves you in return."

"You'll find her when you least expect it, and when you do, you'll know," Ben told him. "The first time we saw Isabel, that was it for us. Just make sure that when you do find her, give her what she *needs*. It may not be what she wants at first, but you'll know."

"The two of you have been waiting a long time for the right woman," Wade added. "You both have so much you have been waiting to give that I think the only problem you two are going to have is that she'll be spoiled rotten."

Clay sat, nursing his drink after the Preston brothers left to deal with their wife, wishing that he had such a problem to deal with. Lost in his own thoughts, he started when his friend Jake pulled out a seat to join Rio and him at the table.

"You guys, okay?"

"Just fine," Clay muttered. "How did it go?"

A jeweler, Jake specialized in pieces not generally found in most jewelry stores. He made most of his money from selling his pieces on the internet.

Jake answered, "Blade came close to losing his temper more than once tonight."

Rio whistled through his teeth. "Blade has more patience than anyone I know. I've never seen him lose his temper in all the years I've known him. What happened?"

Jake poured himself a drink from the bottle on the table. "Two of the Dom wannabes have heavy hands. They also pay no attention to a woman's response. They couldn't tell what pleasured her and what hurt her." His face hardened. "It was Doris. She told Blade that the only reason that she didn't use her safe word was because she trusted him to stop them."

"Son of a bitch." Clay slammed his glass down and the whiskey sloshed over his hand. "I hope Blade and the others can teach them something before they send them back home. I wouldn't want to think what they would do to a woman unsupervised. Is Doris okay?"

Jake chuckled. "She's fine. She stuck it out and will stay the full six weeks. Right now she's being prepared for a trip to the playroom with all three of them."

"Wow!" Rio looked suitably impressed. "She may never leave!"

Jake downed his drink and stood. "I'd love to stay and bullshit but I have to be in Tulsa at seven in the morning."

"Why?" Clay asked as he and Rio also stood. "What's up?"

"Don't you remember I told you about my wife's sister finally coming for a visit?" Jake reminded them.

"Hasn't Nat been trying to get her to come out here for over a year now?" Rio asked.

Jake sighed. "Nat's driving me crazy. She's worried about Jesse. She could never come out because her son was in high school and she couldn't leave him and she couldn't take him out of school to bring him with her. Now that's he's away at college, Nat's not taking no for an answer. She says that Jesse doesn't sound right and she's worried sick. She told Jesse that if she didn't come out here that she was going to Maryland to take matters in her own hands. Jesse finally gave in. Thank God!"

* * * *

Jessica—Jesse—Tyler strode through the airport following the signs to the baggage claim area. She noted several glances cast her way as she moved through the crowd. Just shy of her fortieth birthday, she no longer cared what others thought. She lived her life as she wanted.

She glanced at the mirrored wall as she started past and paused, frowning at her reflection as she wiped a dark smudge from under her eye. At least her skin was good. She owed her creamy complexion and shiny hair to the products she and her business partner, Kelly, made for their store. She looked at her eyes. They looked boring brown and dead. She hadn't seen the gold flecks that made her eyes twinkle when she laughed for a long time. Come to think of it, she hadn't seen anything in them for a long time. Turning away from the depression image, she continued through the airport to find her sister, Natalie.

Before she reached the carousel she heard a squeal. Turning, she found herself enveloped in her sister's hug. Flinching at the unexpected contact, Jesse let herself hug Nat in return.

Releasing her, Nat looked at her sister's face "Jesse! Oh, honey, I thought you would never come! Thank you!" She squeezed her again and Jesse found herself grabbing onto her sister desperately.

* * * *

Jake stayed back and watched as his wife greeted her sister. As a Dom, he'd learned to read a woman's face and body language and Jesse's lack of emotion concerned him, her smile for Nat not reaching her eyes. His gaze narrowed, worried that this cold woman would hurt his wife with her lack of feeling as Nat bubbled with excitement to see her baby sister.

He started forward, intending to issue a low warning until he saw how desperately Jesse embraced Nat. Mmm, something was going on here. Jesse appeared to be hiding something. He planned to keep a close watch on her. If something threatened to hurt his wife, he would take care of it himself. No matter how much Nat loved her sister, Jake couldn't just stand by and watch his wife get her feelings hurt.

He stepped forward as the women separated. "Hi, Jesse. You haven't changed a bit." He took her hand in his, unsurprised when she pulled away almost immediately.

"I have," she admitted. "Life makes you change."

Not commenting, he gestured toward the carousel. "Which bags are yours?"

She waved her claim ticket. "I've got it. Be right back."

"But Jesse," Nat called after her. She looked at Jake in confusion.

"Jesse looks like she's used to taking care of herself," Jake mused as he started after his sister-in-law, his wife in his wake. "She should be used to someone getting her bag, Nat."

He'd lied when he told his sister-in-law that she hadn't changed. She looked colder now than she had when he'd met her years ago.

He'd never made a secret of not liking Jesse's ex husband, Brian. But seeing his apparent affect on her, he knew Brian had a lot to answer for. He just hoped the new, colder Jesse didn't hurt his wife.

If so, he'd have no choice but to step in and he didn't look forward to that.

But watching the way his wife looked at her sister, Jake knew if anyone could help her it would be Nat.

* * * *

Nat closed her cell phone, turning just in time to see Jesse pull the jack out of the back of her car. "Leave that, Jesse. Jake is on his way. Let's go sit in the air conditioning. It's too hot to be doing that."

Nat had taken Jesse to a nearby town to do some shopping, hoping that by being alone she could get some insight into what was wrong with her sister. So far, though, Jesse hadn't talked.

"Jesse, *Please*! Jake will be angry if we don't wait for him."

Jesse looked over at her. "Why would he be angry? I can have the tire changed in a couple of minutes and then he won't have to do anything."

Nat eyed Jesse curiously. "You look like you've done this before. Didn't you call Brian when you had car trouble?"

Jesse pushed the jack into place and started to jack up the car. "Why would I call him when I am perfectly capable of changing it myself? Besides, Brian was never around. Didn't Jake get upset that you called him to come out to change a tire, when he was probably busy? Just call him back and tell him that I'm changing it."

* * * *

"Is that her?" Clay twisted in his seat to see the woman with Nat as Jake made a U-turn.

"Sweet Heaven," he heard Rio murmur from beside him as they pulled up behind Nat's car.

"*This* is Nat's sister?" Clay demanded. "You made her sound plain. She's beautiful."

Jake looked out the windshield. "She is pretty. She's cold, though."

Clay whipped his head around at that. "What do you mean?"

Jake shrugged. "I've been worried that she's gonna hurt Nat somehow. She doesn't seem to have any feelings for anything except her son." He turned to them. "You know how Nat is, always trying to fix everyone. She's gonna get hurt this time and there isn't a damned thing I can do about it." Clay saw Jake's frustration as he regarded his wife. "And why in the hell is she changing the tire when she knew I was on the way?"

Clay heard Jake's frustrated sigh as he watched him climb out of the truck.

Exchanging a look with Rio, he reached for his own door handle and climbed out, frowning as Nat's sister barely glanced at them before going back to work on the tire.

"I told Nat not to call you," Clay heard her say and the soft huskiness in her voice tightened his groin. "I'm sorry to take you away from whatever you guys were doing." She waved her fingers at them. "We'll be fine. This will only take a couple of minutes."

Clay, Rio and Jake looked at each other incredulously.

Jake was the first to recover and moved forward as Clay leaned back against the truck to watch, looking over at Rio to see his brother staring at Nat's sister.

Jake looked at Jesse and frowned. "Are you crazy? Move aside, Jesse. If Nat hadn't called me, her bottom would be so red she wouldn't be able to sit down for a week."

Clay watched Jesse's eyes widen and Nat turn bright red when he and the others chuckled.

But of course Nat didn't back down. "Promises, promises," she told her husband before turning to him and Rio and pouting. "I've been so neglected lately."

He watched Jesse's eyes widen further when Jake murmured, "We'll just have to take care of that when we get home, then, won't we?"

Nat stuck out her tongue at him and turned to her sister. "Jesse, these two intimidating looking men are friends of ours, Clay and Rio Erickson. Clay, Rio, this is my baby sister, Jesse."

Clay moved forward to shake her hand and felt a sizzle of heat run up his arm at the contact. He knew she felt it too by the way she looked up at him, startled and tried to jerk her hand from his grasp. He held onto her hand longer than necessary and watched her closely. The surprise in her eyes turned to panic and Clay couldn't help but notice that her nipples now poked at the front of her baggy shirt.

When he finally released her hand, she jerked it away quickly and watched him warily as she reached out to shake his brother's outstretched hand. He hid a smile when she appeared to have the same reaction to Rio.

She jerked her hand from his brother's grasp, a look of disbelief and panic on her face as she looked back and forth between them.

Her skin was flushed and he didn't think it had anything to do with the temperature. The confusion on her face pulled at him, making her look so lost and vulnerable. She looked bewildered as if she didn't know quite what to make of her response.

He smiled at her mockingly when she crossed her arms over her chest as if to hide the evidence of her desire.

She glared at him.

She certainly didn't look cold to him.

She looked away to say something to Nat and when she turned back she had the cool mask firmly in place. But he'd already seen under the mask and what he'd seen he wanted. Desperately.

When Jesse turned again to Nat, he moved to help Jake. Between them they made short work of changing the tire.

As they worked, Clay studied Nat's sister. Jessica. Jesse. He shot a glance at his brother and saw the same excitement in Rio's eyes that he felt. They had finally found her!

"Jake, why don't you have Nat ride back with you to the house? Rio and I will drop the car off at the garage and pick up our truck in town." He gestured toward Jesse. "We'll bring Jesse back to the house when we're done."

"I was going to stop at the store to pick up some steaks for dinner, though," Nat told them. "If you guys wouldn't mind stopping at the market to pick them up–"

"Not at all," Rio told her, smiling.

"Hey," she exclaimed as though just thinking of it, "why don't you get enough for all of us and stay for dinner? It's so hot, how about if you guys do the grilling and Jesse and I will put together a salad?" She fanned herself. "We're so hot and tired from our trip."

"Sounds good, honey." Jake looked at his wife skeptically. She wrinkled her nose at him.

Clay appreciated Nat and Jake's quick getaway so he and Rio could get Jesse alone before she had a chance to object. When Jesse moved to get into the back, Clay watched Rio edge her toward the passenger seat.

When they both reached for the door handle at the same time, Clay hid a smile as Jesse jerked her hand away and looked at Rio nervously.

Rio smiled at her. "In Desire, women don't open their own doors when a man's present."

When she pushed her hair back from her face, Clay was surprised to see that her hand trembled. She stared at Rio for several long seconds before finally getting into the car.

Chapter 2

Clay drove into town, his attention divided between the road and the temptress sitting beside him. She tried so hard to ignore both himself and Rio. If Jake hadn't warned him of her lack of emotion, he would have been worried. But he had been looking for cracks in her armor and their little darlin' hadn't disappointed him.

He was surprised by the genuine look of surprise when she'd reacted to them. The apparent confusion on her face told him how unfamiliar it had been to her.

It made her response to them that much sweeter.

He hadn't expected to be drawn to the woman that Jake had described to them. He knew from Rio's expression that he felt the same way. He couldn't let her slip away, at least until they could examine this attraction that they felt for her.

Maybe she would be just a temporary diversion for them, but the raging hard-on he had since first laying eyes on her told him that it was something more. And if the way Rio kept squirming around in his seat was any indication, he had the same reaction to her.

"How do you like our town?" He tried to start a conversation.

"It's lovely." She stared out the side window.

"Have you spent any time wandering around town, yet?" He spared a glance at Rio. He didn't want to think about who else she might have met already. When Rio frowned, he knew he had the same unsettling thought.

"No, we spent all day yesterday at the house, then left early this morning to go shopping," she answered, still staring out the window.

Clay had had enough of her trying to ignore them. He reached for her hand, and when she would have pulled back, tightened his grip, careful not to hurt her. "Our town may be a little different than what you're used to."

Stroking her hand with his thumb, he felt the shiver she tried to hide. He grinned.

Jesse wrenched her hand from his. "The town I live in is small. They're all pretty much the same." She tried to hide the tremor in her voice and feared she had failed when she looked up at him. He smiled knowingly at her and she frowned back at him, wondering what in the hell was going on. Feelings she hadn't had in years bombarded her and she wished she could get away from these two until she figured it out.

"Our town is very different." Rio leaned forward in his seat, his breath fanning her ear. "In Desire," his voice lowered, "we absolutely cherish our women. We pleasure and punish them with equal enthusiasm."

Jesse couldn't prevent her gasp as she turned to face Rio. "What do you mean punish them? You hit your women?" she asked incredulously.

"Hit our women?" Clay pulled into the parking lot at the garage and stopped the car. He leaned toward her, crowding her as Rio opened her door, leaning in from the other side. "Not in the way you're thinking."

"What other way is there?" She tried to avoid their touch.

She shivered when Clay reached for a wayward strand of her hair and twirled it around his finger as he looked at her. "For example," he began, "if you belonged to us and you were a bad girl, you could expect to be stripped," as her eyes widened, he continued, "turned over one of our laps with your bare ass in the air, and spanked."

She gasped and knew her nipples could be seen poking through her shirt and moved her arms to cover herself. Clay kept looking at them and smiling. When he touched her arm, she flinched automatically and saw him frown before continuing.

"You would be spanked until your little bottom turned a nice rosy pink, your thighs wet with your sweet juices and you begged us to fuck you."

Jesse stared at Clay in absolute shock. Her heart pounded nearly out of her chest, and if she wasn't mistaken, her panties were wet! Was he for real?

Her gaze spun to Rio to see that he regarded her with the same hot gaze as his brother. As she watched, he moved in closer, "If you were *very* bad," he told her in a voice raw with emotion, "your pleas for release would get you nowhere. At least until you apologized very prettily and promised to behave. And we would have to be sure that your apology was sincere."

Hiding her panic at her body's wild response, she pushed past Rio and got out of the car, vaguely aware that she did only because he allowed it. She had a feeling that as big and strong as these men were, they seemed perfectly capable of holding her however they wanted to. Why did that thought make her panties even wetter?

"All of this means nothing to me since I am not looking for a relationship with anyone." She hoped they'd get the point and back off. "I am curious about one thing, however."

By this time Clay had gotten out of the car and walked around to join them. "What are you curious about, sugar?"

"If the men in this town are like you, why are there any women here at all? They would have left by now. Why would any woman want to be with a man who spanked her?"

Clay and Rio burst out laughing. "Why don't you ask your sister, Natalie?" Clay asked her. "You *do* know that Jake's a Dom, don't you?"

"A Dom?" Jesse looked back and forth between the two men. "You mean whips and chains?"

"Among other things." Clay nodded. "Rio and I aren't Doms like Jake, but we do know how to get our woman to behave. The spanking would let you know that you've crossed the line," he studied her, "but with you, we would be willing to experiment." He looked at Rio. "I never had an interest in using toys on our women, but this one makes me feel adventurous. We've got some shopping to do, Rio."

Rio adjusted his jeans yet again. "Apparently," he muttered.

Clay continued to stare at her and she fought the urge to fidget. "Your sister is getting her ass spanked as we speak, and who knows what else for that little dare back there."

"What dare? She didn't do anything wrong!" Jesse didn't understand why her sister was being punished and worried about her. She briefly pictured the choker Nat always wore and wondered if it was more than just a pretty necklace. Could it be a collar that Jake had put on her?

"Promises, promises," Rio mimicked. "I've been so neglected lately."

Clay smiled and added, "Don't worry about Nat. She's getting exactly what she wanted. She knew how her husband would react. When a man is challenged by his woman, it is his responsibility and privilege to meet that challenge. She wanted her husband's attention, and she got it. Trust me, she'll love it!"

Clay touched Jesse's arm, frowning when she flinched away. "What you need to understand is that the people who live in this town do so for a reason. It was founded by people who had a desire to live their lives in a way that's different from what many consider 'normal'. They wanted to live where they could be accepted, not judged by someone else's standards."

"I don't understand." Jesse shook her head in confusion. "Do you mean that a lot of Doms live here?"

Clay nodded. "Yes, and there are a lot of men who are like Rio and me. We want a life where we have a woman who loves both of us and who we both love. Our parents lived the same way. We grew up in this town. We always knew that we wanted to live our lives that way."

"We've both been married before," Rio added. "We married two different women and hated it. We've both been divorced for some time now and are ready to get on with our lives. But this time, we're going to live the way we've always wanted."

Clay nodded and continued, "The point is that the people here live their lives in the way that suits them and nobody gets judged. We get women who are subs coming here looking for the right Dom. There are also men and women living in this town as couples, who simply like the town. It is just as normal to see a married couple in this town as it is to see a collared woman with her Dom or a woman with more than one husband."

Jesse couldn't help but be intrigued. "But, having more than one husband is illegal," she argued.

"In the eyes of the law, yes," Rio told her. "In Desire, a woman is legally married to the oldest, whether it is brothers or just friends, but a ceremony that includes all parties involved is performed. We have a woman in town named Isabel, who is married to three brothers. She is legally married to Ben, who is the eldest, but if anyone dared to insinuate that the other two aren't her husbands, there would be hell to pay. She loves all three of them and they worship the ground she walks on. That's how it is here."

"It works here for us," Clay added, "because we *make* it work. There are a lot of unwritten rules here that newcomers learn in a hurry, and abide by, or else they get run out of town."

"Unwritten rules?" Jesse couldn't help asking. "Like what?"

"The first rule," Clay told her "is that the women are never harmed. Anyone who hurts a woman gets the shit beat out of him and becomes an outcast. We are all very close knit here and an outcast could never survive."

"I like that rule." She nodded. "What else?"

Clay seemed happy that she showed an interest in their lifestyle and continued. "Another rule is that you have to listen to the men around you, or your husbands will be told that you disobeyed and you will be punished."

"That's not fair." She shook her head. "Why should a woman have to obey every man in town? That's ridiculous!" She turned away but stopped short when Clay grabbed her elbow.

She turned back to snap at him but stopped when she saw the pleading look on his face.

"Try to imagine this town over a hundred years ago, Jesse. Doms and men like us, men who wanted to share a woman founded this town. Do you know how hard it was for women back then? They had no rights and no choice but to obey their husbands. They could even be beaten!"

Jesse saw his grimace and Rio's and was heartened by it. "So the women who came to Desire back then couldn't be beaten?" She found herself intrigued by the thought of people moving here at a time when their lifestyle choices would have been frowned on by society.

Clay shook his head. "If a man beat his wife, he became an outcast and would be forced to leave. The town allowed his wife to stay where she would be safe and protected. You have to understand, Jesse. The women had more freedom here than most of the women in the country. How could a town grow if women wouldn't come here, feeling they would be mistreated by Doms or multiple husbands? These rules *protect* our women. They still do today."

"Think about it from the other side, Jesse." Rio smiled at her. "The rules keep the men in line. Do you have any idea how hard the people in this town would come down on a man for beating or even cheating on his wife?"

Clay nodded. "Look, no one but your husbands would tell you what to do but if you found yourself in a position that was dangerous or could cause you harm in any way, another man would move to protect you. We *all* protect *all* of our women at all times. If you disobeyed him, he would get you out of harm's way and take you to your husbands."

"Then," Rio added, "you would be severely punished by your husbands for not seeing to your own safety."

"Well since neither of those rules applies to me, I'm not worried about it." She moved toward the garage. "We'd better go inside and tell them about the car."

"Oh, but these rules *do* apply to you, darlin'," Clay told her.

Jesse stopped abruptly and turned. "Since I don't have a husband, I fail to see how any of this applies to me."

"You're staying at Jake's house, aren't you?"

"Yeah, so? What does that have to do with anything?"

"Well as long as you're under his roof, he's responsible for your safety."

"What?" Jesse flung her hands. "That's ridiculous!"

"When in Rome, honey." Rio chuckled.

"I'll tell you something else you don't know." Clay frowned. "Jake has every right to turn you over his knee for trying to change that tire. You could have been hurt."

At her gasp, he added, "How do you think Nat would have taken that? I'll bet she tried really hard to get you to stop trying to change that tire, didn't she?"

Jesse's flushed guiltily. "Then, Rio and I would have been really upset that someone other than the two of us had spanked your ass. Consider yourself lucky that we got there before you could do any damage, and the fact that Nat distracted him."

Jesse turned and strode ahead of the men as she headed for the open garage bay, their words still ringing in her ears. For someone who had trouble feeling anything, her system felt bombarded from so many different angles that she couldn't process it all.

Entering the garage she stopped short at the sight of a tight butt and muscular thighs lovingly encased in a pair of well worn, faded jeans leaning over the front of a car. She watched as those muscles shifted as the man who owned them straightened when he heard their approach.

Jesus, was every man in this town tall and gorgeous?

He smiled at her mischievously as he took in her loose fitting jeans and oversized T shirt, his gaze making her aware of the fact that he knew what she tried to hide in such ill fitting clothing.

She felt no desire to dress revealingly, to attract unwanted male attention. It certainly seemed to make no difference to these men.

Clay moved to stand in front of her, his large back like a wall blocking her view of the mechanic and her from his.

Jesse could no longer see the mechanic but when she heard him ask "Who's the pretty lady?" She managed to nudge Clay aside.

What was wrong with him?

"Hi, I'm Jessica Tyler, Natalie Langley's sister."

As she reached to shake his hand, she felt Rio brush past her and offered the mechanic his own hand, effectively keeping the man from touching her.

"Hey, Ryder. We've brought Nat's car in. She had a flat so we put on the spare but she needs a new tire."

Shaking his friend's hand, Ryder nodded. "No problem." He turned to her and smiled. "So, you're Nat's sister? How come I've never seen you before?"

"I've never visited before." She carefully put space between herself and the men. The testosterone level rose and she became absurdly aware of her body's response. This was getting out of hand.

"I wondered if you could check out the fan belt while you had the car here. It seemed to be making some noise," Jesse said. At the men's surprised looks, she continued, "I don't know a lot about cars, but when mine made a noise like that, the mechanic told me it sounded like a fan belt."

"She's right." Clay frowned. "I was going to ask you to look at it."

"Will do." Ryder nodded. "Tell Jake I'll call him tomorrow. Do you guys need a ride?"

"No, thanks." Clay shook his head, still eyeing her. "My truck is parked in front of the market. That's where we all were when Jake got Nat's call." He reached for her hand. "Come on, sugar, let's go get those steaks."

Jesse turned to say goodbye to Ryder, surprised to find him smiling flirtatiously at her. "It's been really nice meeting you, Jesse. I hope you come back and see me before you leave. I know Dillon would love to meet you, too."

"Who's Dillon?" she asked.

"Dillon's my partner," Ryder told her with a wink.

"Oh, that's nice," Jesse smiled. She assumed Dillon and Ryder were a gay couple and was glad that they could be happy in this town. She was taken aback when both Clay and Rio burst out laughing.

Ryder chuckled, shaking his head, and moved closer to Jesse, totally ignoring their glares. "Not that kind of partner, sweetheart." His voice lowered. "Dillon and I are partners in the garage, but also when we take a woman to bed."

Jesse looked up at him in surprise. Remembering what the men had told her out front, she couldn't resist glancing at them, surprised to see fear in their eyes as they regarded her steadily. Did they think she would fall into Ryder's arms? If she could have laughed, she would have.

"Ready, sugar?" Clay asked, extending his hand again.

Without thinking, only knowing that she wanted to wipe that look from his eyes, she placed her hand in his. Murmuring goodbye to Ryder, she turned and allowed Rio to take her other hand as they left the garage.

Walking the two blocks to the market, Clay and Rio holding her hands, she struggled to make sense of all this. Looking around them, she saw other women with more than one man. Remembering their earlier conversation, she looked for and found several women who wore collars, some with a man, some not. She carefully checked out the people she saw, surprised that almost every woman looked deliriously happy.

It also surprised her that the looks the men gave their women appeared to be lovingly indulgent. The men held the doors open for the women, helped them to cross the street with a hand on their arm or on their backs, carried their packages. Every man acted like a gentleman.

She realized it had been a long time since she had seen people acting this way and had never realized it.

Before she knew it, they had reached the market. She pulled her hands from theirs, automatically reaching for the door handle. Suddenly remembering Rio's words, she paused.

"Good girl," he crooned, making her shiver. "You remembered."

As he opened the door, she shot him a wary glance and brushed past him. Clay, with a hand on her back, guided her inside.

Shopping with them was a nerve-wracking experience. They touched her at every opportunity. Clay crowded her as he reached over her head for the apple juice she wanted. Rio steadied her with an arm around her waist as she reached for produce. She never even noticed when she stopped flinching at their touch.

* * * *

Clay wanted to shout for joy as little by little she allowed their touch. Soon their little darlin' started to become aroused and he wanted to kiss her little frown as she appeared to finally realize it.

Always getting in her way soon had her eyes flashing gold sparks. She might put on a cold front but he'd bet the ranch that inside her an inferno raged, just waiting to be tapped.

But although she slowly became accustomed to their touch, she still wouldn't talk. She deftly avoided all personal questions about herself which made Clay want to put her over his knee. The hard-on he had been sporting since laying eyes on her jumped to attention at that thought. Great! At this rate he would have to excuse himself to jerk off before he could sit at the table with her.

He had only known her for a few hours and he was ready to explode. He saw his brother's strained features whenever he touched Jesse and he assumed the same tension showed on his own face. If they didn't make this woman theirs soon, they may both just burst.

He no longer doubted that this was the woman he and Rio had been waiting for. He couldn't believe that she'd finally arrived, and couldn't wait to start their lives together. But, the sadness and distance in her eyes had to be dealt with.

As soon as possible.

Chapter 3

When they pulled up to her sister's house, Jesse could see the smoke and knew Jake had already started the grill.

As they walked in the door, Nat handed her a margarita.

"Jake never makes these for me anymore, but when I told him how much you love them, he made us a pitcher."

Jesse took the glass from her sister and followed her to the kitchen. Sipping at her drink, she helped Nat with the dinner preparations.

Several minutes later, standing at the sink washing the vegetables for the salad, Jesse watched as Nat crossed the yard with a platter full of steaks. Clay said something to her as she handed the platter to her husband. Whatever she replied caused both Clay and Rio to frown. They glanced at the window where Jesse stood, their eyes hot even at this distance.

Nat appeared fragile and delicate as she stood next to the three men. They all looked so big, especially Clay and Rio who stood even taller than Jake. She'd found herself watching their hands while in the grocery store, imagining what they would feel like on her body. They'd both touched her and rubbed against her over and over and her nipples still actually ached with the need to be touched by those large hands. Their arms, well muscled probably from years spent working a ranch would hold a woman securely, making her feel safe and warm.

Now where had *that* come from?

Shaking off her fanciful thought, Jesse continued washing vegetables watching as Nat talked to the men. Jake shook his head in amusement at whatever she'd said, his love for Nat apparent in the look he gave her.

Apparently finished, Nat turned away from the men, jumping in surprise when a grinning Jake smacked her sharply on her ass. Nat turned, and with a hand on her hip stuck out her tongue at him. Jake said something to her, his expression stern as he pointed at her. Seemingly unfazed, Nat laughed and turned back toward the house.

Over dinner, and after two margaritas, Jesse started to relax and enjoy herself. As the meal progressed it got easier to let Clay and Rio fuss over her as Jake fussed over Nat. Conversation flowed as they ate. Jesse was quiet as she watched and listened, noting how close they all appeared to be. The camaraderie showed clearly as they spoke of others who lived in Desire with fondness and laughter.

When they had all finished with their meal, Nat and Jesse rose to take care of the dishes, waving off the men's offers to help.

"Sweetheart," Jesse smiled as Nat cuddled closer to Jake, "would you please make us another pitcher of margaritas?"

"I think I've had enough," Jesse told Nat with a smile. "I don't think Jake would appreciate having to deal with a drunken sister-in-law."

"Nonsense," Nat told her. "Besides, you and I haven't sat and talked alone in years. The guys will be outside dealing with the grill and if we get falling down drunk, they'll take care of us. Jake won't make another pitcher, though, unless you're sharing it with me. He knows my weakness for margaritas."

Since any further objection would disappoint her sister, Jesse gave in. With the dishwasher running the women sat alone at the table, fresh drinks in front of them. The men could be heard out back, their voices low through the open window.

Nat kept Jesse talking about the business she and a friend started back in Maryland, steadily getting her baby sister more than a little tipsy. She knew Jesse didn't drink much and would soon be loose enough to talk. She felt a little guilty about her devious method of finding out what was wrong with Jesse, but she had to hurry. She only had two weeks with her sister and in the last two days had been unable to get a thing out of her. She wanted to help her, to try to fix whatever was wrong and bring back the Jesse she had grown up with, and her sister's uncooperative silence seriously hindered her efforts. Taking matters into her own hands seemed to be the only way.

Clay and Rio had objected at first, but when they realized how much she wanted to help Jesse, they relented, provided they could eavesdrop in the hope of finding a way to get closer to her.

Jesse sipped at her drink as she told Nat about her business back home.

"Kelly works mostly on the formulas while I deal with the sales and package designs," she told Nat. "We make everything ourselves, using all natural ingredients. We started out making hand cream, but now we also make shampoo, conditioner and bath oils."

"Is that the stuff you've been using that makes you smell so great?" Nat asked enthusiastically. "You always smell like peaches. I think Clay and Rio would love to take a bite!"

Jesse grimaced. "That can't happen, Nat." She finished her drink, carefully placing the glass back on the table, her movements more and more deliberate as the alcohol took effect.

"I brought stuff with me for you. I should go get it." Before she could stand, Nat stopped her.

"Later, let's just sit and talk."

"It makes your skin sooo soft," Jesse breathed. "And we have the most incredible powder." She sipped her drink, and then frowned.

Nat watched Jesse smile and wondered if her sister realized she'd refilled her glass.

"This new powder tastes like it smells. I wear the peaches and cream." Hearing groans, she blinked in confusion. "What was that?"

"Just the dishwasher acting up, Jake promised to look at it," Nat answered, raising her voice so the men could hear. If they wanted to eavesdrop the least they could do is be quiet.

"I'd love to try the powder. I'll bet Jake would love it!"

"It also makes your skin look all drewey, er dewy," Jesse corrected herself. "I brought you the cinnamon spice. I thought it would shoot you, er, suit you."

Realizing that Jesse had had enough, Nat took the half full margarita pitcher to the sink and poured it down the drain. She didn't want her sister to get sick, just *very* loose. Looking out, she saw that the three men sat at the table below the window, apparently listening to every word.

Turning back to the table, she sat and regarded her sister, who had her head resting on her folded arm as it lay on the table. "What made you and Kelly decide to start a business?"

"I got tired of wearing panties with holes in them," Jesse answered tiredly.

"Excuse me?" Had Jesse had too many margaritas?

"Did you ever notice how sexy it sounds when a man says the word panties?" Jesse mused. "Brian called them underwear. Men wear underwear. Women wear panties!"

Nat knew her sister well enough to follow and agreed. "Yep, you're right. When Jake says anything with the word "panties", I get all riled up."

"There you go." Jesse nodded, and then continued, enunciating carefully, "Anyway, Brian always had a get rich quick scheme. They never worked. Neither did he." She sat up and looked around, frowning at the glass of water that sat in front of her.

"So, you started a business," Nat prodded.

"Nope, cleaned hotel rooms. My hands used to get so dry and cracked but I didn't have the money to spend on hand cream, not with buying new clothes for a constantly growing boy." She sat quietly a moment, apparently remembering that time, her face looking so forlorn that Nat wanted to hug her. She watched as Jesse seemed to shrug it off. "Kelly made me some. Others liked it, so we decided to start making it and selling it."

"What happened with Brian?" Nat asked, knowing that he had something to do with how Jesse had changed. "I never did like him and Jake hated him on sight."

"I'm frigid, you know?" Jesse told her sister matter of factly. "Don't feel much of anything anymore. Get hurt enough, I guess it closes down."

Nat stared at her sister in shock. "What are you saying, Jesse?"

"Brian never loved me, Nat," she told her sister stoically. "He never held me. He never touched me unless he wanted something from me, usually sex." She leaned forward. "I see how Jake is with you."

Jesse appeared to be only slightly sober, but the words kept spilling from her.

"Jake's always touching you, playing with your hair, even when you're just sitting there watching television." Jesse gestured wildly. "Jake touches you because he wants you and loves you. Brian made me feel like the man, Nat, and I don't know how to be a woman anymore."

"Oh, honey!" Nat jumped up and ran to kneel by Jesse. "Of course you're a woman! How could you think otherwise?"

"Oh, Nat, you could never understand! Not being married to a man like Jake."

"Explain it to me then, Jesse. Make me understand."

"Oh, Nat, in the beginning, it used to be awful. It just got worse until one day I realized I had finally become used to it. Brian didn't like to work, so I had to. All through my pregnancy, I worked cleaning hotel rooms. After I had Alex, I took him with me." Smiling sadly, she continued in a low voice, "He went everywhere with me while Brian ran around in thousand dollar suits charged to my credit card and met with 'investors'."

Rubbing her hands over her face, Jesse continued, "He was so lazy, Nat. He didn't do anything except dress in fancy suits and expensive jewelry and meet with people he conned money from."

Jesse sipped her water and leaned against Nat.

"I took out the trash. I locked up the house at night. I cut the grass, shoveled the snow, learned how to fix the plumbing and all the other things that a man is supposed to do around the house."

Shaking her head sadly, she told Nat, "I'm not lovable."

"Jesse, that's not true!"

"Even my own husband didn't love me." When Jesse turned to face her, Nat wanted to cry. "He never initiated sex because it wasn't worth the energy to try to arouse me. He would just get really mean sometimes, and I would think, 'How long has it been since we had sex last?' When I realized it had been a couple of weeks, I would have to ask him if he wanted to have sex. It was the only way to get peace in the house."

Her eyes stayed flat as she continued, "He would, of course, say yes and then just sit there. I had to play with his cock until it got hard." Swallowing hard, she played with her glass, not looking up.

"Then I would take off my panties and bend over. Thank God it didn't last longer than a minute or two. When he'd finished, I pulled on my panties and went to get cleaned up."

When she tried to stand to refill her glass with water, Nat nudged her back in her seat to get it for her.

Running the water, Nat looked out the window into the agonized expressions on the men's faces. Clay and Rio looked like they wanted to kill somebody and Jake didn't look much better.

Jesse's sad voice carried to the window. "I haven't been kissed or held in so long, Nat."

Nat couldn't stand anymore. With a last glance at Clay and Rio, she returned to the table, determination in her step.

"Honey, Clay and Rio would love to kiss you, among other things. I want you to give them a chance."

"I can't, Nat."

"Why not? Those two are crazy about you already. I want you to at least spend some time with them."

"What would be the point? Don't you understand? I can't laugh. I can't cry. Not with anyone, except Alex. With anyone else, the rest is dead."

"It is if you're going to keep barriers between you and the rest of the world," Nat argued.

"You still don't understand." Jesse sighed tiredly and Nat's heart broke. "It isn't a choice for me. I don't know *how* to take the barriers down. They've been a part of me for so long. I just don't know how to feel anything anymore."

"Bullshit!" Nat stood with her hands on her hips and regarded her sister. "Are you trying to tell me that you didn't feel anything for me when you hugged me at the airport?"

Jesse blinked in surprise.

"You forget how well I know you, Jesse. A person doesn't change that much. You're not Brian's Jessica anymore! You're Jesse, damn it!"

"Nat, you don't understand."

"Oh, I understand very well," Nat told her. "I saw the way you've been watching them. Did you think I missed the way you reacted to them this afternoon? I saw you get all flustered. You looked more alive than I've seen you since you got here!

"Do you think I didn't see how you blushed every time one of them looked at you or touched you at dinner? I saw the way you kept staring at their lips and licking yours. I saw the way you stared at their hands. You imagined them on you, didn't you? I may be older than you, honey, but I'm not old. They interest you and whether you want to admit it or not, they arouse you."

Jesse could feel her panic building. Jeez, have a few drinks and open your mouth and look what happens. She began to suspect Nat had an ulterior motive for having Jake make those margaritas.

Angry now, she turned on her sister. "Damn it, Nat! What am I supposed to do? Just spread my legs for them? Have a fling and move on? Do you really think that men like that are going to be happy fucking a woman who can't come?"

"Men like what?" Nat asked.

"Like them!" She gestured to the back yard. She hoped they couldn't hear them. Since she hadn't heard the men's voices for quite a while, she assumed they must have gone somewhere else. "Have you looked at them? I know you love your husband but you can't be blind! Clay and Rio are drop dead gorgeous. Big and strong and muscular with asses you just want to take a bite out of!"

Nat smiled that knowing smile that she'd always worn whenever she'd won an argument. "Welcome back, Jesse, I've missed you."

Jesse blinked in surprise.

"You're crazy!" Jesse smiled indulgently at her sister, then quickly sobered. "This is just the margaritas talking. I'm different now. Nat. If I couldn't please that lazy excuse for a husband I had, what makes you think I'm going to be able to satisfy *two* men who can have any woman they wanted?"

Nat smiled and leaned toward her. "Clay and Rio are strong men with hearts of gold. They have been looking their whole lives for a woman they could both love and who would love them both in return." She chuckled. "They haven't been celibate, not by a long shot. I have seen them with a lot of women over the years, and I have never seen them look at a woman the way they look at you. Not even their wives. Maybe you're the one for them and they're the ones for you, maybe not. But, don't you think that the three of you owe it to yourselves to find out?"

"In less than two weeks I have to go back home."

"Maybe, maybe not."

"But I can't just leave Kelly alone." No matter what, she couldn't desert Kelly.

"We'll worry about that later." Nat regarded her closely. "Now, I'm going to do something that may make you angry, but I'm doing it for your own good."

Nat reached for her hand, pulled her out of the kitchen and headed for the stairs. Jesse was pulled up the stairs and into the guest bedroom where her sister began repacking her suitcase.

"Are you throwing me out?"

"Not quite." Nat went into the adjoining bathroom for Jesse's toiletries. "Where's my cinnamon stuff? I can't wait to try it out on Jake."

Wondering what her sister could possibly be up to, Jesse went to the closet to retrieve the purple bag. Eyeing Nat closely, she handed her the bag, watching her struggle to close the suitcase. Nat had never been able to pack a bag.

When Nat finally got the suitcase closed, she hugged Jesse, whispering in her ear, "I love you, honey, remember that."

Jesse regarded her sister suspiciously, starting to get really nervous. Following Nat back down the stairs and walking into the kitchen, she stopped short. Clay, Rio and Jake sat at the table drinking coffee as though they had been there all along. Glancing at the window, she saw that it had been closed. Nat must have closed it when she refilled her water. The men couldn't have heard their conversation, she thought with relief.

Jesse looked at Nat. "I don't understand, Nat. What are you up to?" She never trusted her big sister when she got that look on her face.

"Clay, Rio, I'm giving Jesse to you," she heard her sister say.

"What!" Jesse gasped, looking at Nat.

Nat ignored her. Looking sternly at the two grinning men, Jesse heard her say, "I'm trusting you with my sister. I trust you not to hurt her. If everything goes well, you have to have her back to me the day before she is *supposed* to leave to go home. I want some time with her. Since I'm giving you most of it, I expect you to respect my wishes. If things don't go well, bring her straight back to me." She looked like a drill sergeant as she paced in front of the men. "Not to the airport, no matter what she says, but straight here to me."

Jesse stood, shell shocked, as she watched Clay and Rio take turns hugging Nat. She heard Clay murmur, "I love you, Nat." Rio took his turn hugging her sister. "Thank you, honey. You won't be sorry."

Jesse took a step back as they approached her, eyeing her intently. She'd never been so scared in her life!

Clay reached for her while Rio picked up her luggage.

"Wait." Jake stepped forward.

Thank God. Jake would be the voice of reason and get her out of this. Going away with these two men would be like a fantasy in one of the books she loved to read. She always read about ménages and thought it had to be the greatest fantasy on earth, to have two men completely devoted to a woman's happiness, but until today, she never realized that people actually lived like that. But, she couldn't stay and living the fantasy and destroying it would be worse than not living it at all.

Expecting Jake to put an end to all this, she turned toward him and found herself embraced in his strong arms. Then he surprised her. He held her arms, regarding her closely and she wondered briefly what he saw that made him nod.

"I know this isn't what you want right now," he told her, dashing her hope of a rescue. "But, I think Nat's right. You'll be seeing a lot of Nat and I while you're with Clay and Rio. I insist on it." He gave the men a warning look.

Turning his attention back to her, he smiled. "If, at any time, you want to come back here, you tell me. I want you to try, though, honey, okay?"

Jesse could see why Jake would be a good Dom. He could talk a woman into anything.

Knowing she could leave whenever she wanted gave her courage. She would try her best not to destroy this fantasy. She nodded hesitantly, "Okay."

Looking out the corner of her eye and seeing the satisfied smile on Clay and Rio's faces, she hoped she was doing the right thing.

"Good girl." Rio smiled mischievously.

Jake turned to his friends. "Now for you two, I'm trusting you with my sister-in-law who's under my protection. You know that I take that responsibility very seriously. Are the two of you willing to take over as her protectors for as long as she stays with you?"

"Absolutely," Clay answered. Reaching out to touch her hair, his eyes never leaving hers, "It would make both Rio and I very happy to be Jesse's protectors."

"We promise to take very good care of her," Rio added, smiling at her.

Nat smiled as she watched the men hurried her sister out the door. She knew the men would be good for Jesse if she would only give them a chance.

The Jesse she'd grown up with could light up a room with her smile and had always been full of mischief. Marrying that jerk had certainly changed her and Nat wanted the old Jesse back. Clay and Rio may just be the men to do it.

Watching Clay's truck pull out, Nat leaned back contentedly against her husband's strong chest. "I think they're just what she needs, and she's just what they need."

She grasped his arms as his hands slid under her top. Flicking her bra open, his hands closing over her breasts, he whispered in her ear. "You're just what I need."

She moaned as he pinched her nipples. God, she was wet already. It amazed her sometimes that after being married to this man all these years, he could still make her wet with a touch, a gesture, a word spoken in a voice that never failed to arouse her. He used it now.

"And," he whispered darkly, "I know just what you need."

"What?" she gasped as his hand deftly unzipped her jeans and slipped inside.

"You need to be spanked for lying about the margaritas. I make them for you whenever you ask and you told your sister that I never did. You've been a bad girl."

Nat gasped again as his fingers pushed into her sopping wet pussy. "I'm really sorry, but I wanted to loosen her up a little. She wouldn't have had any if she didn't think you had made them for her. She wanted to please you."

"How about you?" He yanked the top over her head and pulled her bra off. Picking her up in his arms, he headed toward the bedroom. "Do you want to please me, too?"

"Oh, yes!" Nat wound her arms around her husband's neck and nuzzled his jaw. "What can I do to please you?"

Dropping her on the bed, he quickly dispensed with her jeans and panties. Flipping her over onto her stomach, he held her still with a large hand on her back. "You can stay still while I insert the new butt plug I bought for you today." She gasped and heard his chuckle. "You'll have it in while you get the spanking you deserve." He nuzzled her neck. "It's larger than the one I've been using on you."

She tried to jump up and felt his hand firm on her back.

"Jake, no! That one's big enough!"

She watched as he reached for the lube and felt him lean on her back as he lubed his fingers. She heard the tube hit the nightstand a second before he pulled her to him, flipped her around and settled her over his knees.

"Are you going to try to tell me what size butt plug you need for punishment, now?"

"I'm sorry," Nat whimpered, gasping again as two lubed fingers entered her anus.

"You're going to be sorry, sweetheart," Jake promised.

Nat shook so hard with excitement that she knew that the only thing that kept her from falling off her husband's lap was his strong grip on her. She could feel his fingers slip out of her then a cold hardness at her most vulnerable opening. He knew how turned on she got when he did anything to her anus, the feeling of helplessness at any intrusion into her ass making her feel small and vulnerable while he effortlessly held her in place. He took great delight in playing with her ass and she knew that the spanking would be more intense while he filled her with the plug.

He would move the plug around in her for the duration of her punishment, and she knew that seeing a plug in her ass while he spanked her spurred him to become more dominant than normal. And that was a lot.

Knowing that he watched as he pushed the plug into her anus, she knew that she could be in trouble tonight. He would spank her for longer than normal, and at times like this, when he pushed her further, she knew she would also be getting her pussy spanked. She almost came at the thought.

"Are you ready for your punishment, my darling little sub?" His voice sounded raw with emotion.

"Always my love, my master." She opened her legs wider for him and felt the burn as the large plug pressed into her.

Chapter 4

Jesse was settled securely between Clay and Rio as they started toward their home. With both being so broad shouldered, they crowded her in her seat. Instead of feeling cramped, she felt small and feminine and protected. She absorbed the sensation and wanted to remember how wonderful it felt when she was back at home and lonely.

She liked this feeling but still wondered how she had allowed herself to be manipulated into going with Clay and Rio to their home. She wanted to blame it on the margaritas, but deep down she knew that she craved male attention brought to the surface by her reaction to these men. Scared of what this might lead to, she couldn't ignore the sexual pull as they led her into their web.

She had never had such feelings with any man. Not even her husband had made her feel this way before they got married. Something warmed inside her and she started to feel hope that she wasn't doomed to remain this cold unfeeling creature that she had become.

Looking up at Clay, she felt her nipples harden. He kept glancing at her as he drove, the heat in his gaze unmistakable. She felt the moisture flow from her pussy, amazed again at how much these men affected her.

"We're glad you're coming with us, honey." Folding his much larger hand over hers where they clenched on her thighs, he let his fingers trail over the inside of her thigh, grazing her jeans over her pussy.

"Thank you for giving us a chance to see how good we can be together." His smile told her he knew the effect his hand had on her.

Feeling the need to warn them, Jesse looked straight ahead and began, "I think there's something you should know about me before this goes any further."

"What's that, darlin'?" Rio asked.

"I'm not good at sex," she blurted before she lost her nerve. She continued to stare out the windshield, not having the courage to see the disgust she knew had to be written on their faces. "I don't want you to take it personally, I mean don't blame yourselves if I can't, er, you know." She knew her face turned bright red as she continued to stare straight ahead.

"Come?" Rio asked pleasantly.

"Yes." She nodded. "I usually don't like to be touched. It turns me off. With you, though, it seems to be different, but I'm not used to it." She glanced up at Clay. "I'm not sure what will happen if your touch gets more intimate."

She turned even redder as both men laughed. "Oh, our touch is going to get a helluva lot more intimate," Rio warned.

"Step one," he continued, "seems to be getting you accustomed to our touch. While you're staying with us, will you agree to let us do whatever has to be done to explore your boundaries?"

"Before you answer," Clay added, "be very sure, because if you say yes, you're saying yes to us doing whatever we want to do with you, touching you everywhere. If you truly don't like something, we'll stop, but if you're creaming like you are now, we're going to keep going no matter what you say."

Rio gently turned her to face him, his fingers gentle on her chin. "It's all about your pleasure, honey. Our pleasure depends on your pleasure." She gasped when his thumb caressed her bottom lip. "So, what's it gonna be? Will you agree? Will you trust us with your body, with your pleasure?"

Inhaling deeply, she whispered, "Yes," before she could change her mind. Without thinking, she touched her tongue to Rio's thumb. Startled at herself, she tried to pull back.

"Oh, no, you don't." Rio pulled her onto his lap, her back against his door. "You said yes, and teased me with that little tongue. You're all ours now, darlin'."

With that, he began to kiss her, his tongue sweeping into her mouth in a kiss like none she had ever had before. He tasted like sin as he teased and cajoled with his tongue, urging her to play with him. His fingers pulled up her top and unhooked her bra until her breasts were free for both of them to see.

"Beautiful," she vaguely heard Clay as Rio continued his devious assault. He broke the kiss to pull her top over her head and remove her bra. Running his hands over her breasts, he murmured to Clay, "Feel how smooth and soft she is."

He continued to explore a naked breast while Clay reached over for his own inspection. "Baby, your breasts feel so good, soft here," he circled her breast with his callused hand, "and harder here." He tweaked a nipple, and then pinched it lightly between his thumb and forefinger.

Jesse arched as Clay and Rio continued examining her breasts, lightly pinching and pulling on her nipples as they tried to see what she liked. "Oh, God," she whimpered. Riding along in a truck, half naked while two gorgeous men played with her breasts had to be the most mind blowing experience that she had ever had. Highly aroused, she didn't even care if anyone saw her.

Jesse felt a hand undo the snap on her jeans. Rio kissed her, his hand on her breast as she felt the zipper being lowered. Rio lifted her and she felt her jeans being pulled off. Clad now in only a pair of cotton panties, she felt vulnerable and grew hotter.

She felt a hand, she didn't know whose, and didn't care, lay over her mound. "Your pussy is really wet, sugar." She heard Clay's voice, the tension in it unmistakable. "It's so hot, maybe we better get these panties off."

The way he said "panties" caused her to cream even more. She soon became soaking wet and started to feel a little embarrassed at it. She heard a rip and felt her panties being torn from her. She thought it impossible to get any wetter. She closed her legs as she felt the air from the window on her wet folds.

"Uh, uh," she heard Clay scold. "I want those thighs wide open." Moaning into Rio's mouth, she felt Clay pull her left leg until her foot touched his headrest. Rio meanwhile lifted his mouth from hers and moved her right leg until her foot pushed against the dash board.

With her legs now splayed wide open, Clay had a good view of her pussy. His eyes darkened even further as he reached for her, running his fingers through her soaked folds, then spearing a large finger inside her.

Lying naked, spread wide, with Clay and Rio's undivided attention, she felt more desirable than she had ever felt in her life. They appeared to be mesmerized by everything about her, a balm to a wound she didn't realize was so raw.

She shook so hard with desire now that she would gladly do whatever they asked of her if only they would hurry and do something! She wanted to be fucked as she never had before.

"Please," she whimpered, past caring how wanton she sounded.

"Please, what, baby?" Clay asked deviously.

He knew just what they had done to her, damn it, and more than aware of the effect it had on her. His finger was in her pussy, for Christ sake. He knew the height of her arousal and still he continued to tease her. She moved restlessly on his finger and their wicked grins told her they enjoyed the show.

"You have got to feel how tight she is," Clay told his brother. He pulled his finger out of her and almost immediately she felt another push into her.

She heard Rio moan. "If her pussy is that tight, can you imagine how tight her ass is gonna be?"

"What!" Jesse tried to close her legs to no avail. Both men had a grip on her and she couldn't move anywhere. "I don't do that!"

"Do what, darlin'?" Rio asked. "Don't get fucked in the ass?"

"I've never been taken there," she admitted, then gasped and arched again as Clay touched her clit. "Like that, baby?"

Her mind went blank as Rio continued to stroke her pussy, adding another finger as she heard him tell Clay that she needed to be stretched a little more. She felt the truck stop, and glanced out the window to see that they had pulled up in front of a two story house.

Her eyes closed again as Clay turned in his seat, keeping her legs parted for their touch. He teased her clit mercilessly, circling it until she moved to try to make contact with his finger. He avoided her easily, making her sob in frustration.

"Have you ever had anything in your ass?" Rio asked, hoping her arousal wiped out embarrassment. "A finger, a butt plug, anything?"

"Nooooo! Please, please, please! I'm ready. You don't have to wait."

Rio looked over to see Clay looking as angry as he felt. Remembering what Jesse had told Nat about her sex life, he knew she had never been played with like this. She'd obviously never had this kind of attention, had never been aroused to this extent and they had only just started.

He watched as Clay touched his finger to her clit and gave her what she craved. She arched and came in complete abandon, beautiful as her skin flushed a rosy pink. She screamed, and then whimpered like a kitten as his brother brought her down gently. He wished he could have had his mouth on her but with no room to maneuver in this damn truck he knew that it would have to wait. He would, though, he promised himself. He couldn't wait to get his mouth on that hot pussy.

He had only intended a little petting on the way home, but their little darlin' had gone up in flames. She responded so well to every touch that it surprised him that he hadn't come in his jeans. Watching her come had been more arousing than anything he could remember. Already beautiful to him, when she came she blew him away. He wanted to get his mouth on that pussy. He loved to eat pussy, and since he and Clay had all but claimed her for their own, his desire to taste her grew even stronger.

He couldn't imagine anything better than the taste of his woman's pussy.

He wanted to shove his cock inside her so deep that she would feel it in her throat. But, as tight as she felt, he and Clay would have to be gentle with her as they stretched her to accept them. They would get Jesse so hot, she would beg them to fill her.

Rio strode into the master bedroom and noticed Clay pulling down the bedding with a flick of his wrist. He looked down at the tempting bundle in his arms, completely naked, her skin flushed a rosy hue, and grimaced as his jeans became even more uncomfortable.

Laying his precious bundle on the cool, crisp sheets, he stood and tore off his clothing, his eyes never leaving the beautiful woman on the bed. Jesse eyes widened as she watched them undress, starting to look a little nervous as she saw them naked for the first time.

Rio saw how Jesse's eyes moved back and forth as she watched him and his brother undressing. He couldn't wait to sink into her, any part of her, and he knew by the look on his brother's face, that he felt the same.

But, after hearing what that bastard of an ex-husband had put her through in the bedroom, he knew they would have to go slowly; arouse her again thoroughly until she begged to be taken.

Clay shifted, drawing Rio's attention and, out of Jesse's sight, reminded his brother with a gesture that they had to slow down. Rio nodded and took a deep breath before reaching for her.

* * * *

Jesse could hardly believe this. She had just had the most incredible orgasm of her life, still weak from it as she watched Clay and Rio undress. She shifted, uncomfortably aware of how wet she was and embarrassed. She wanted a few minutes alone.

She asked the only thing that came to mind. "Can I take a shower?"

"Later, baby," Clay promised. "Rio and I will give you a bath."

No one had bathed her since she'd been a little girl and she wasn't sure she would be comfortable with being bathed by Clay and Rio. But all thoughts of a bath went out of her head as they finished undressing.

Dressed, they were intimidating. Naked, they were lethal. She knew that both Clay and Rio were older than her own almost forty years, but not an inch of flab could be seen on them anywhere. Years of working their ranch showed in the way their muscles shifted as they moved.

Clay removed his boxers and Jesse's eyes widened as she took in his size. She wondered frantically how she would be able to accept him into her body. He looked thicker than her wrist and long. She had thought of Brian as average, but he was tiny compared to Clay.

She glanced over as Rio's boxers came off and moaned. Almost as thick as Clay, his cock looked even longer.

"I don't think this is going to work," she blurted nervously.

Clay and Rio looked at each other and smiled at her reassuringly.

"We're going to fit inside you like a hand in a glove, baby," Clay promised as he brushed her cheek with his thumb and moved in, taking her lips in a kiss so possessive and hungry it curled her toes.

Clay's kiss proved to be just as intoxicating as Rio's, but where Rio's lips had been teasing, Clay's demanded. His tongue swept through her mouth, tangling with hers, possessively exploring, demanding a response Jesse couldn't withhold.

He lifted his head to gaze at her hungrily. Jesse lifted her hands to his dark hair, grasping handfuls of its thick silkiness, absently tracing her thumbs over where she knew a few strands of silver shone.

As he lowered his head to her breast, scraping her nipple with his sharp teeth, she felt Rio move between her thighs.

She sucked in a breath as Clay nipped and sucked at her breasts, using his lips, his tongue and his teeth, thoroughly exploring them, seeming to gauge her response to every touch.

Rio parted her folds with his thumbs, making her squirm. She didn't think it possible to get aroused again so soon after having such a mind-blowing orgasm.

"I'm gonna lap up this sweet pussy, darlin'," she heard him say even as she felt him part her further, her legs over his broad shoulders, keeping them open.

Clay paused and looked over his shoulder and watched Rio lower his head to Jesse's pussy. He heard Jesse's gasp as she jolted in his arms when Rio's tongue swept through her folds. He watched her eyes glaze over with passion as Rio used his mouth, thoroughly exploring the woman that they had been looking for all their lives.

He heard Rio moan and knew his brother was enjoying his first taste of their woman. He felt Jesse writhe in his arms as Rio used his mouth on her, smiling when he saw his brother slide his hands under her bottom and lift her more firmly against his mouth.

Clay moved to kneel on the bed, one hand stroking his throbbing cock and with the other he reached out to cup Jesse's cheek. When she looked at his cock and licked her lips, his cock jumped.

"I want my cock in your mouth," he told her.

She gasped, opening her mouth and Clay moved closer.

"Will you teach me how?" she asked, looking up at him.

Clay saw Rio lift his head and knew that he'd heard her, too. When Jesse smiled at him shyly he felt his cock jump again.

"Baby, have you ever had a cock in your mouth?"

"No. I never wanted Brian that way."

"Open your mouth, baby." Clay rubbed the head of his cock on her lips. He wanted to push himself all the way into her hot mouth. Knowing that he would be the first almost set him off but he gritted his teeth against it and soon had himself under control, barely.

"Darlin'," he heard Rio as he pushed the head of his cock between her soft lips, "Has anybody but me tasted this sweet pussy?"

Clay moaned as Jesse shook her head, her mouth rubbing against the head of his cock. He looked over to see the incredulous pleasure on Rio's face. He knew just what his brother was thinking. Jesse's sexuality had barely been tapped. The woman writhing helplessly under their hands and desperately trying to suck his cock into her untutored mouth had almost no sexual experience.

It would be up to them to teach her everything. She had been fucked, but never taken in the ways that Clay and Rio planned to take her. She was aroused, but it was nothing next to what they would do to her. She had never been fussed over the way they wanted to pamper her, and she had never had her man spank her if she disobeyed them.

All the things they had done with women over the years would be brand new again as they taught their woman. She belonged to them.

Her hot mouth drove him crazy. He'd become too aroused with his cock in her mouth for the first time to be able to show her anything, and this time he didn't need to anyway. What she didn't have in experience she more than made up for in enthusiasm.

Clay felt ecstatic that she responded so well to them. He'd become so aroused by their woman that he struggled to maintain some kind of control when he wanted nothing more than to devour her whole. Glancing at Rio, he saw that his brother appeared just as taken with her.

Jesse felt Rio position himself at her entrance and trembled in anticipation. She wanted him inside her so badly, wanted them both more than she could ever dream she'd want a man.

She took as much of Clay's cock into her mouth as she could and tried to squirm onto Rio's but he held her still.

"I'm gonna fuck this hot little pussy, darlin'."

She heard Rio's voice over the loud groans that filled the room and wished he would hurry. His shallow thrusts gained ground with each thrust but she wanted it all.

Now!

Jesse had never felt so wanted in her life, had never felt so feminine as she took Clay's and Rio's cocks. Clay's taste filled her with heat and she couldn't get enough of it. His response to having her mouth on him drove her wild.

She felt powerful and wicked as she used her tongue on him and tried to suck him as far as she could into her mouth. She heard his moans and felt his hands tighten on her as she sucked him deep, wanting him to lose the control she knew he was trying so desperately to hold on to.

She arched as Rio fucked her. She couldn't prevent the constant moans coming from deep in her throat as Clay and Rio drew responses from her that had lay dormant for years.

Every inch of her body hummed. She arched, forcing Rio's cock further into her dripping pussy and groaned at the fullness.

"Easy, darlin'," he said from between clenched teeth. "I don't want to hurt you."

She squirmed restlessly and sucked harder at Clay. She burned and needed more and tried to move but Clay and Rio easily controlled her.

She felt Clay tighten and try to pull away. She sucked harder and scraped her teeth warningly over his cock, ignoring his tense "Fuck!" Her hands tightened on him, one holding the base of his cock, not allowing him to pull away and the other cupping the full sack between his thighs.

She felt his fists tighten in her hair. "Baby, I'm gonna come. Let go," he growled.

As Rio pushed his full length into her, Jesse doubled her efforts and she heard Clay moan.

"Fuck," she heard Clay bite out as he filled her mouth with his seed. Swallowing frantically, she continued to suck every bit from him as he stroked her hair.

"You're amazing, baby," he crooned, pulling out of her mouth to move beside her on the bed. He leaned over to kiss her, his lips biting hers erotically. "You are going to be punished for not letting go when I told you to, though. Rio and I want to watch you come again, baby. You belong to us now, don't you? Give it to us."

Jesse heard Clay's words as Rio pushed deeper inside her. The full feeling had her trembling helplessly.

"Darlin', you feel fantastic," Rio groaned. "You're so tight!"

"Harder!" Jesse pleaded. She was so close. As Rio continued his slow smooth strokes, Clay's mouth on her breasts tormented her further.

"I don't want to hurt you, darlin'." Rio held her hips firmly in his strong hands, not allowing her to push his cock deeper as she writhed, desperate to come.

Her clit throbbed. When she felt Clay's hand cover her abdomen, she whimpered.

"Please! I need more. Touch me!"

Clay lifted his head and his eyes met hers. She saw the tenderness in their depths as she felt his fingers move lower.

She knew when Rio's control finally snapped. His thrusts became harder. His hands tightened on her hips. He buried himself to the hilt inside her, his cock hitting her womb. She came in a fierce orgasm that wrung a scream from her, frightening her with its intensity. She dimly heard Rio groan as he pounded into her.

"Fuck," he panted. "Her pussy's milking my cock. So fucking hot!"

He surged into her with one last powerful thrust, holding her hips firmly in place as she felt Clay's touch on her sensitive clit.

"No more! No more!" Shaking her head weakly, she lifted her hand toward Clay. She felt Rio's pulsing cock splash his seed deep inside her as Clay's fingers moved on her clit.

"Once more, baby," she heard Clay croon. Grasping her outstretched hand firmly in his, he and Rio wrung another rippling orgasm from her.

* * * *

Jesse never wanted to move again. She felt more sated than any self-induced orgasm had ever made her feel. Her ex-husband's quickie, selfish sex had never even come close to arousing her, let alone leaving her feeling completely drained.

Clay and Rio lay on each side of her, tenderly stroking her rapidly cooling body. Rio nuzzled her neck while Clay placed soft kisses on her face and shoulders. Their lips didn't demand as before but felt just as possessive. Their murmured endearments and praise washed over her.

She felt enveloped in a warmth she had never felt before by these two strong sexy men who made her feel like the most beautiful, desirable woman in the world. A sense of coming home, the absolute rightness of being with Clay and Rio filled her.

Tears stung at her eyes at the joy that swept through her. The only time she had ever felt like this had been when she'd held her son for the first time. Feelings she thought Brian had killed rose up from somewhere deep inside her, bursting through and stealing her breath.

Relief that she could feel again and the intensity of her feelings toward the doting men on either side of her, seeing to her comforts even after the sex, had the tears in her eyes spilling to run down into her sweat drenched hair.

"Baby?" Clay rose to lean over her, pushing her damp hair back from her face. Rio quickly joined him, rubbing her stomach.

The concern and tenderness on their faces as they cuddled her snapped her self control and with a strangled sob, she broke.

Through her tears she saw the startled panic on her lovers' faces and sobbed harder. She felt Clay pull her effortlessly into his arms as tears flowed down her face and sobs shook her body.

"Baby, please tell us what's wrong," Clay pleaded. He rocked her and she felt Rio's hands as he rubbed her back and arms.

"Did I hurt you, darlin'?" She heard the desperation in Rio's voice and wanted to reassure him but couldn't speak through her tears. She reached for him, her face still held against Clay's chest. She felt her hand being gripped in his and she squeezed.

She felt as though her heart would burst from her chest. She gasped for air as her sobs wracked her body uncontrollably. Being cold and numb for so long, the warm rush of feelings for these men hurt.

Desperate to get away, Jesse pulled her hand from Rio's and pushed at Clay's chest. He merely tightened his hold to keep her in place. Panicked, she started to fight him, nearly hysterical now as she fought to get free. She wanted to bolt, to lock herself in the bathroom until she could get herself back under control.

As Clay tightened his hold, he continued to rock her.

"Please, baby," he murmured, "tell Rio and me what's wrong. We'll fix it, I promise."

"Come on, baby," Rio added. "Please stop. I can't take it when you cry."

"Please, let, let me go," Jesse hiccupped.

"Never!" Both men protested in unison.

"Rio, go draw a bath for her." Jesse felt Clay's lips on her hair as he continued to rock her. "She's going to make herself sick, crying like this. We've got to get her calmed down."

Jesse finally managed to stop sobbing and felt Clay lift her in his arms. She fought to control the tears still running down her face. Embarrassed, she hiccupped against his chest as he carried her into the bathroom.

Rio stood waiting for them, filling the huge tub, the peach scent she used filling the air. He'd obviously gotten the things from her bag and it touched her that he'd thought of it.

When Clay carried her into the bathroom, Rio held out his arms for her, smiling at her tenderly.

"Let me hold her."

Jesse found herself being transferred to Rio's arms. He held her tightly to his chest as he lowered them both into the warm water. Clay sat across from her, rubbing her feet as he watched her.

The warm water felt wonderful. So did the arms holding her so securely.

Jesse let her head fall back on Rio's chest. The sex and the crying had worn her out.

She knew her face was red with embarrassment. Clay and Rio must think she's crazy.

She had to get away, go back to Nat's then fly home. The men once so anxious to take her to bed had to be just as anxious to get rid of her.

She tried to keep her head lowered, too embarrassed to look at their faces, but Rio wouldn't let her. Pulling her face from his chest, he began wiping it with the warm washcloth.

"I'm sorry," she hiccupped. "Please take me back to Nat's."

"Why, Jesse?" Rio brushed the hair back from her face. "Tell us what happened. Please tell us what we did wrong."

His eyes shone with tenderness and concern, which caused tears to well up again.

"Darlin', were we too rough? Did we hurt you? Scare you?"

Jesse shook her head, surprised that they thought they could have been anything but wonderful with her. "No, you didn't do anything wrong. It's me." Reaching up, she held his face in her hands and touched her lips to his.

"I'm sorry I cried like that." She glanced at Clay to see that he watched her hungrily. "I never cry. It must have been uncomfortable for you. I'm really sorry. Please just take me back to Nat's. We can forget this ever happened."

Jesse winced, taken aback by the anger that jumped into Rio's eyes.

"Clay already owes you a spanking for what you did to him in the bedroom." Rio held her chin forcing her to look at him. "You didn't make us uncomfortable. You scared the shit out of us. We want to know what happened to make you cry like that. If you don't tell us right now, I'm going to turn you over my knee and paddle your ass until you do."

Jesse pressed a hand to her stomach as nerves made it jump. She doubted that he would actually spank her but the look on his face told her that he wanted an answer and his patience had worn out.

She looked beseechingly at Clay who met her gaze steadily, lifting a brow as she continued to stare. No help there.

She looked back at Rio. "I don't know if I can explain it."

"Try." Rio's voice brooked no argument.

She squirmed in his arms, pushing against his chest. He reluctantly let go, as if sensing that she needed the space. He gave her some, but not too much as he held on to one of her ankles, stroking tenderly.

"Come on, baby." Clay ran a hand comfortingly over her calf.

"It just got to be too much," Jesse whispered and took a deep breath. "I haven't felt so much in such a long time, I guess it kind of overwhelmed me."

She looked up at them, meeting their gazes steadily. "It's like being cold for so long that you become numb to it. You don't realize how cold you've become until you're covered by a warm blanket." She swallowed the tears that threatened again.

"*You* were the warm blanket. It hurt after being cold for so long, and I guess it kind of scared me." Her eyes went back and forth between them. "I didn't think it would be like this. I can't stay here. I have obligations at home that I can't walk away from."

Clay pulled her to him, nestling her between his thighs and she leaned back against his chest.

"We'll work everything out, baby." Clay started washing her with the shower gel Rio must have found in her bag, handing Rio the tube. "You're exhausted. Just relax and let us take care of everything."

Rio washed her legs, moving upward as Clay lathered her breasts, her nipples plainly visible through the suds.

"I don't want to get hurt," Jesse whispered reluctantly.

Clay pulled her hair back until her head rested on his shoulder. "We're not about to hurt you, but we're not willing to let you go, either."

His lips met hers as he ran his hands over her breasts, the soap making them slippery.

"We're crazy about you, darlin'." Rio's fingers slipped to her folds.

"You don't even know me," she protested, then gasped as their wicked hands bathed her.

"We know you well enough," Rio assured her. "We started to fall for you the moment we saw you and we've been falling ever since."

Clay rinsed her and methodically washed the rest of her and she felt her eyelids begin to droop.

"We also know that you're tired and too sore for anything else tonight."

They finished bathing her, even washing her hair. Rio dried her and rubbed her peach lotion on her skin while Clay showered. Clay dried her hair while Rio showered, then carried her naked into the bedroom.

When Jesse fell asleep, her head on Rio's shoulder, Clay met his brother's eyes over Jesse's head and saw the supreme satisfaction on Rio's face. He knew the same look had to be on his own. He had never felt such complete happiness in his life.

Their loving gazes caressed the woman between them, the woman who had already imbedded herself in their hearts.

"I love her already." Rio's said softly.

"I know." Clay's said just as softly. "She's perfect." He sighed in contentment as Jesse turned in her sleep toward him and he pillowed her head with his shoulder. "Thank God we finally found her."

Chapter 5

Jesse woke the next morning to the smell of coffee. She stretched languorously, groaning as sore muscles protested. Smiling as she remembered why, she opened her eyes. And grinned.

Rio sat on the side of the bed next to her, a cup of coffee in his hand. He smiled when she looked at him.

"Good mornin', beautiful." His lips felt warm and tasted of coffee as he nuzzled hers tenderly, pushing her hair from her face.

"We've decided to keep you." He watched her face intently as though trying to gauge her reaction.

"Don't scare her off, Rio." Clay stepped into the room with a cup of coffee in each hand. He eyed her tenderly but she could feel his scrutiny as though trying to see how Rio's declaration affected her.

"Have some coffee, baby." He leaned over for a tender but possessive kiss, his tongue sweeping her mouth before he straightened and handed her a cup.

Jesse felt like a queen, being fussed over like this. "I don't think I've ever been served coffee in bed before." She grinned at both of them. "I could get spoiled."

"If you stay with us darlin', we'll spoil you rotten." Rio grinned at her.

"Rio, if you scare her off, I'm gonna kick your ass." Clay's said softly but with a warning bite. He turned to Jesse.

"We have a lot to do today. Finish your coffee and get ready to go. We'll grab breakfast in town."

"Where are we going?" Jesse sipped her coffee, surprised to find it exactly the way she liked it. She had thought that Clay and Rio would want to stay in bed this morning, but they both seemed to be in a hurry to go out. Excitement lit their eyes and she hoped it had something to do with her. She could get used to the feeling of being wanted.

She reluctantly reined in her thoughts. She couldn't stay. She couldn't live here happily knowing she had left Kelly defenseless.

Determined not to let anything spoil her time with Clay and Rio, she slid naked from the bed, carrying her coffee with her to the bathroom.

"I'll be ready in twenty minutes," she tossed over her shoulder. She shook her head when she caught them both looking at her ass.

* * * *

Breakfast at the diner with Clay and Rio taught her a lot about the town, and them.

The diner seemed to be more like a family gathering than the diners she had eaten in back home. Everyone seemed to know everyone else and laughter filled the room.

She and the waitress, Gracie were introduced and she couldn't help but be surprised to learn that the three men in the kitchen were Gracie's husbands. Three husbands!

Of course everyone knew Clay and Rio and greeted them warmly. Jesse found herself introduced to several of Clay and Rio's friends and neighbors. Most smiled indulgently when they saw how both men acted with her, touching her, keeping her close, their eyes tender as they smiled at her.

To her surprise, Jake and Nat joined them. Glancing at Clay and Rio she saw that both had been expecting them.

"We're spending the day at the spa!" Nat told her as soon as she sat down.

"What are you talking about, Nat?" Jesse accepted the toast Rio had buttered for her while Clay refilled her coffee cup.

"There's a wonderful day spa at the end of town," Nat told her excitedly. "We're spending the day there."

Jesse shook her head, hating to disappoint her sister. "I can't afford something like that, Nat."

"We're paying for it, baby." Clay sipped his coffee. "Don't worry about it."

He resumed eating while Jesse sputtered. "What? You're not paying for anything!" She rounded on Rio as he opened his mouth to speak. "I'm not going to a spa. That's final!"

Several heads turned at her outburst and Jesse saw that several of their friends had turned to look at Clay and Rio. She dropped her head and hissed at them. "If you don't want me around, that's fine!"

She cursed the tremor in her voice and squirmed when both Clay and Rio sat up straighter and looked at her.

Jesse bit her lip as she gathered her things. Stupid. Stupid. Stupid. Of course they wanted to get rid of her, otherwise they would have kept her at their house with them.

"I have things to do today anyway. Maybe I'll see you around."

She stood and found herself immediately surrounded by two very large, very angry men.

"Sit down, Jesse." Clay's hand on her arm firmed but it was the steel in his voice that had her lowering back into her chair.

Clay and Rio leaned in close, filling her view with their frowning faces.

"We are *not* trying to get rid of you," Clay gritted through clenched teeth.

"You promised that you would do what we wanted," Rio reminded her. His face hardened but his eyes remained tender. "We want you to go for a couple of hours with Nat. The people at the spa know exactly what we want done to you."

Jesse couldn't prevent the shiver that went through her at Rio's voice and mischievous smile.

"What are you talking about?"

"We want you to relax and be pampered while we do some shopping for you," Clay told her, sending Rio a warning glance.

"Shopping for me? For what?" Jesse eyed them warily.

"We'll explain everything tonight." Clay patted her arm, straightened in his chair and sipped his coffee. "Just relax and enjoy yourself with Nat. Tonight you'll be busy."

Jesse leaned closer to Rio, noting the surprise and pleasure in his eyes as she did.

"What did you tell them to do to me at the spa?" she whispered worriedly.

Rio chuckled and dropped a quick kiss on her pouting lips. "You're getting your hair done, a facial, massage, manicure, pedicure, the works. We want you to feel pampered, which you probably have never been in your life."

Rio leaned close and nuzzled her ear and she shivered. "We're also having you waxed darlin'."

When she would have pulled away, she felt his teeth close on her earlobe, effectively keeping her in place. When she stilled, he released her with a soft chuckle.

"Tonight when I put my mouth on your pussy, it's gonna be smooth and bare."

He moved to see her face and she noticed that Clay still watched her, his expression amused. His eyes held hers as Rio murmured quietly.

"With your pussy bare, it will be so sensitive. Clay and I are gonna spend a lot of time with our mouths on your pussy and clit, driving you crazy."

Breakfast resumed as though nothing had happened. Everyone ate ravenously except her. She picked at her food while the conversation flowed around them. She noticed that several of the men raised their coffee cups in salute to both Clay and Rio. What was all that about?

"Idiots," Clay mumbled under his breath and Rio and Jake laughed.

She didn't pay much attention. She was too busy trying to rein in her response to them. She felt her nipples harden and become more sensitive and she had wet panties. Again.

These two knew just what buttons to push to keep her almost constantly aroused. Buttons she didn't even know she had. It creeped her out that these two seemed to know her better than she did herself.

She still felt uncomfortable with the way she had fallen apart last night. Neither of them mentioned it, but she saw the knowledge in their eyes and felt it in the possessiveness in their touch.

She frowned, disconcerted to be so vulnerable. Even more so to feel the way she felt about not one, but *two* men at once and she hadn't known them for twenty four hours!

"Heavy thoughts, sweetheart?" Clay lifted her chin until her eyes met his. When she saw the concern in them she shook her head and smiled.

"No, nothing." His concern melted her heart. She couldn't do anything about it. She had fallen for them. She could only enjoy it while they still wanted her.

His raised brow told her he knew that something bothered her but he let it go for now. Jeez, they noticed everything. That kind of attention would be hard to get used to.

After breakfast Jesse left with Nat in Jake's truck for their trip to the spa. Jesse's lips still tingled from Clay's and Rio's goodbyes, which let her know just how anxiously they anticipated her return.

"Do you ever get used to it?" Jesse asked Nat curiously.

"Get used to what?" Nat glanced at her.

"The way Jake treats you." Jesse turned in her seat until she faced her sister. "I mean, he's always touching you, kissing you, looking at you like he can't wait to get you alone. You've been married for over twenty years and you act like you're newlyweds."

Nat laughed. "I have to admit, when Joe still lived at home, sometimes it got a little hard to have sex like we wanted but now that he's working in Tulsa, it's been like starting over."

She looked at Jesse and teased. "The three of you are going to have a lot of fun getting to know each other since your son and theirs are all away at school. When they come home for vacations, you'll be so frustrated that when they leave again we probably won't see you for days!"

Jesse smiled. "They told me about their boys this morning. They sound like good kids, but I can't stay, Nat. Hey! Pull over!"

It looked perfect. As Nat stopped the car, Jesse scrambled out. Excited, she pulled Nat along when she joined her on the sidewalk.

"Look at this!" Jesse eyed the old building with awe. Cupping her hands around her face, she peered in the window.

With her mind racing, she pulled a small notebook from her purse and jotted down the number for the leasing agent.

"Jesse, what's going on?" Nat looked from the quaint old building to her sister.

Jesse looked around, noting the parking available and the other shops in the area. She saw a florist, a woman's apparel store, a beauty salon, a movie theater and a bank among others. Jake's jewelry store stood on the corner.

She knew that the garage they had taken Nat's car to stood only a few blocks away along with the market. It looked like a lovely town with clean sidewalks and flowers and trees planted everywhere.

"Jesse, damn it. What's going on? What are you doing?" Nat demanded, grabbing her arm.

"Nat, what would you think of me moving here?" Jesse asked.

"Oh, honey! That would be wonderful! Do you mean it?" Nat laughed excitedly.

Jesse frowned. "I'm not sure that it's going to work out with Clay and Rio or not, but I think I like it here. Kelly would be safe." She paced up and down the sidewalk as she thought about it.

"Nat, Kelly needs to get out of Maryland. The reason it took me so long to come visit is because Kelly's ex boyfriend likes to show up now and then and beat on her."

"What?" Nat gasped, outraged.

"Please don't say anything to anyone. I don't want everyone to know Kelly's business."

"Oh, no!" Nat assured her. "But if you can get her to move here, I want a front row seat if this asshole shows up thinking of hurting her." Nat paced angrily. "Clay, Rio and Jake would clean his clock, along with any other man around here."

Jesse shook her head. "I don't want anyone fighting. I don't think he'll come here. He's a friend of Brian's. That's how Kelly and I met."

Leaning against Jake's truck, Jesse folded her arms. "I've managed to take care of him so far."

"What do you mean?" Nat asked, frowning at her.

"He's not very big, only a little taller than me. He's also as lazy as Brian so he's out of shape. I've worked like a dog for years doing my stuff and Brian's. I'm in better shape than he is." She shrugged. "Once when he came after Kelly, I happened to show up. He was surprised. I was pissed. I won. Since then, I make it my business to be around Kelly as much as possible. Every time he shows up, I'm there and I think he's scared of me."

Shaking her head, Jesse straightened. "I want to call the leasing agent. Then, I'll talk to Kelly. I want to have a plan before calling her. Since Alex left, I've wanted to leave, but I just can't leave Kelly alone. This may be my chance."

"Oh, Jesse. It would be great if you could move here." Jesse followed as Nat gestured toward the building. "This would be a great location for your business. There isn't another business like it in town so you should be able to get approval. We don't like it when a new business runs another out of town, so we only allow one to come in if it's different. No one else will be able to compete with you. And the women in town are going to love your lotions. I went nuts over the stuff you gave me." Nat smiled mischievously. "And so did Jake."

Jesse nodded thoughtfully. "I just wonder if there are enough people in this town to support a store here though."

"Jesse, you have no idea of the amount of business our town gets from all over. Jake's jewelry store, the club's seminars, Beau's adult store, the bar, Logan's leathers and Preston brother's furniture all bring a lot of business to the town. We all help each other."

Jesse looked at her sister in surprise. "I didn't realize. I haven't seen these places."

Nat laughed. "Unless I'm very wrong, I'm sure Clay and Rio are hitting a few of those places today buying things for you. They're probably like two kids in a candy store, finally having the woman they've been waiting for all these years to buy for."

Jesse wondered what they could possibly be buying. Meeting Nat's eyes, she raised a brow. "Like what?"

"No way!" Nat laughed and rounded the front of the truck. "I'm not getting into this conversation. I'm not sure what Clay and Rio would buy, but I would guess lingerie is included."

"Great," Jesse sighed. "Something that I'm sure to look ridiculous wearing. I usually sleep in a big cotton shirt, Nat."

"I'm sure you'll look great in whatever they get," Nat told her confidently. "Especially after the spa! Get in or we'll be late."

"Promise me you won't say anything about this place or my plans," Jesse demanded after they'd climbed into in the truck. "I don't want Clay and Rio to feel like they're stuck with me. I want to live here even if things don't work out with us. I'm not even sure if Kelly would move out here. I can't leave her defenseless, Nat. Her brother is visiting her now which is why I could come."

"I won't say anything, but Jake doesn't like it when I keep things from him." Nat shook her finger at Jesse. "You'd better come clean before either of us gets into trouble."

"*I'm* not the one married to a Dom." Jesse grinned. "Besides, when he finds out that you kept something from him, he might just give you a nice spanking. I'm doing you a favor."

Nat laughed as she put the truck in gear. "There is that!"

Chapter 6

Leaving the spa several hours later, Jesse felt better than she had in years. Clay and Rio waited outside for her along with Jake who waited, tapping his foot impatiently, to take Nat home.

Jesse felt relaxed and pampered, her nerves soothed, but she bubbled with excitement at the prospect of spending another evening with Clay and Rio. Knowing that they had spent the day preparing for tonight increased her anticipation.

She had already spoken to the leasing agent and found the lease not only affordable, but also included the apartment above. She and Kelly would have a place to live close to work.

Everything seemed to be falling into place and she felt more excited about the future than she had since before her marriage.

Hugging Nat goodbye, she waved at Jake before being turned and lifted into Clay's embrace. Her whole body tingled with desire. "I missed you," she heard him say as he nuzzled her neck before tilting his face and taking her lips with his.

Incredible heat raced through her body. His mouth both enticed and possessed, sweeping her quickly to a burning arousal. Her nipples pressed against his chest and her newly waxed pussy dripped with her juices.

She felt the heat surround her as another hard body pressed against her back. Rio cupped her bottom as he swept her hair aside and nipped the back of her neck, immediately soothing the tender skin with his lips and tongue.

"Let's get the fuck out of here," Rio growled as his hands came around to cup her breasts.

Clay lifted his face from hers. "You drive," he told his brother as he set her carefully in the front seat and scooted her to the center until she sat firmly settled between them.

She loved being surrounded by their large bodies, their heat. Reminding herself that this could be temporary, only sex, depressed her.

When a strong pair of hands grasped her shirt, ripping it open, sending buttons flying, she forgot about her depressing thoughts.

"You ripped my shirt," she accused, trying hard to look stern.

"I'm going to rip all of your ill fitting clothes off of you," Clay threatened darkly. "Rio and I bought clothes for you today, among other things. You'll wear what *we've* bought you, nothing else."

"Or what?" She tried to sound tough but feared that she didn't quite pull it off. His low voice along with the way he traced her bra cups with his finger had her breathless already. "What if I wear my clothes?" Damn, did he hear the tremble in her voice?

"We'll rip them off you." Clay pulled the torn shirt from her. She knew they had turned onto the back road that was rarely traveled, but still nervous about being seen wearing only her bra. Okay, topless, as she felt Clay remove her bra.

"What if someone sees me?" She couldn't prevent asking and frantically covering her breasts with her hands.

"No one will ever see these pretty breasts except Rio and me," he told her forcefully, pulling her across his chest and lifting her breast to his mouth.

His mouth felt hot on her nipple, his teeth sharp as he tormented her mercilessly. She felt her womb clench and her clit throb with the need to be touched.

She reached down to rub herself through her jeans but found her hand caught in Rio's before she reached her destination. She moaned in frustration.

"Uh, uh, sugar." Rio folded her hand in his much larger one. "Your days of pleasuring yourself are over." He chuckled when she tried and failed to pull her hand from his.

Clay lifted his head and cupped her jaw, turning her until she faced him.

"I already owe you one spanking, which you're going to get as soon as we get home." He grinned when her eyes widened and she glanced nervously between him and Rio. "You didn't think I forgot about it, did you?"

One strong arm at her back held her in place as his other hand tugged at her nipple. "God, you are so soft. I can't wait until Rio and I get you naked."

He shook his head to clear it. "Christ, you go to my head faster than aged whiskey. When we get you home, you're going over my knee for the stunt you pulled last night. I wanted to come in your pussy the first time, not in your mouth."

She gasped when he pinched her nipple. "You're going to learn that we mean what we say. No more pleasuring yourself. If you need to come, one or both of us will satisfy you."

He ground his mouth on hers as he continued to torment her breasts. By the time Rio parked in front of the house, she'd been reduced to a bundle of quivering need.

Clay carried her quickly into the house and straight to the bedroom where he laid her on the bed and began tugging at her jeans while Rio pulled off her shoes and socks. In seconds, she lay naked.

Clay and Rio's gazes locked on her now bare pussy. Each reached for her dripping folds.

"Oh, my God!" Rio breathed harshly as he ran his fingers over her.

Clay's fingers joined his brother's on her pussy and she felt him push inside her. "She's so soft." He ran a finger up to circle her clit. When she jolted, he chuckled. "More sensitive, too."

He lifted her. "Come on, baby, time for your spanking."

He pulled her struggling form easily over his muscled denim clad thighs, a hand on her back holding her in place.

Jesse couldn't move no matter how hard she tried. She tried to squirm, nervous and embarrassed beyond belief.

And very, very aroused.

She had never been over anyone's lap before and knew that they could see her most private places while she lay helpless to cover herself.

When Rio knelt next to her thighs, her sense of foreboding increased. "What are you going to do to me?"

She cursed herself for the quiver in her voice.

A sharp slap landed on her rear. She couldn't prevent the squeal that escaped. More slaps followed and she squirmed uselessly, cursing at them both. Clay held her securely just the way he wanted her and it appeared she could do nothing about it until he decided to let her go.

The warmth from her bottom spread. To her utter surprise and mortification, she became even wetter. She felt her juices on her thighs. Her pussy dripped.

Squeezing her thighs together, she moaned as Clay's hand smoothed over the flesh his hand had warmed. She felt his hand push between her thighs. "Open your legs, baby."

Embarrassed that he would feel how wet his spanking made her, she tried desperately to hold her thighs together. Another sharp slap on her bottom made her jump.

"Open!" Rio demanded and pushed his hand so they each pulled on her thighs, parting them.

Clay chuckled and dipped two fingers into her soaked pussy. "Somebody enjoys getting a spanking." He stroked her pussy and she let her thighs part further to give him better access.

"Oh, oh, please," she begged.

"Not yet, baby. Soon," he promised.

She heard a drawer open and felt Clay's fingers slide out of her.

"No!" she sobbed. She felt him part the cheeks of her bottom and froze in surprise. A cold wetness touched her anus and she squealed again. She felt Clay's finger push the lube into her anus.

"No!" Panicked, she tried to get up but Rio held her down with a hand on her back.

"Stay still, darlin'. We have to stretch you before we can take your ass."

"Stretch me? Take my ass?" Jesse squirmed in both fear and excitement.

Rio moved forward and pushed the hair out of her face. "We don't want to hurt you, darlin'. When we take you together, you're gonna come like never before."

He rubbed a hand down her back. "And so will we." His eyes darkened with emotion and lust. "We've waited our whole lives for you. Let us make you feel good."

Jesse nodded hesitantly. "I'm scared," she admitted tremulously, not used to any of this.

Rio grinned deviously. "I would be if I were in your shoes. You're just gonna have to trust us."

Rio moved away, back to kneel at her thighs. "I'm gonna watch while Clay opens your tight little bottom, darlin'. I wouldn't miss this for the world."

Jesse could feel her face flame as Clay opened her ass cheeks wider. "The problem with you, baby, is that you've never had a man who could handle you."

He pushed one of his large fingers past the tight ring of muscle and fully into her and she gasped. "Now, you have two of them."

Jesse felt his finger slide into her. She felt the pinch and unfamiliar fullness of her rear being invaded. He stroked slowly in and out, working the lube into her.

"Oh, God!" Jesse felt her thighs being parted and a hand, it had to be Rio's, slip between them. A rough finger circled her pussy opening and she felt him push into her.

She automatically pushed back against him, inadvertently pushing Clay's finger further into her ass. The feeling, uncomfortable and unfamiliar, quickly became forbidden pleasure, her inhibitions disappearing as she opened her thighs wider. What Clay and Rio did to her amazed her. She had never had this much attention paid to arousing her.

She felt Clay pull his finger out of her and tried to follow it. She wanted to come!

"Please, don't stop! Put it back!" She heard them both chuckle, too aroused to care.

"Let's try two fingers. Then I'm gonna put the small butt plug inside you."

"Butt plug?" Jesse asked warily.

"Rio and I did a lot of shopping for you, baby. Now, let's see how well you take two fingers."

Jesse felt Clay push more lube into her and his fingers press firmly against her tight opening.

"It burns!" Jesse panted as Clay pushed relentlessly into her anus. She never felt so vulnerable and couldn't believe that this helpless feeling made her even hotter. She would bet the two of them knew it though.

Clay held her ass cheeks open and she knew both he and Rio watched as Clay's fingers stretched her. They had completely taken over her body until she no longer felt in control of herself.

She moaned as Clay continued to press into her, stretching her. The painful pleasure felt so foreign she struggled against it, more than a little afraid of how much it affected her.

"It's too much!" She protested even as she pushed against Clay's hand, taking his fingers further into her. "Oh!"

When Rio's fingers slipped from her pussy to circle her clit, she jumped.

"Easy, baby." Clay held her firmly in place as he continued stroking her. His cock throbbed, rock hard as he worked her ass, knowing how tight and responsive she would be when he finally worked the length of his cock into her tight bottom.

Her juices wet his jeans, her arousal so great at whatever they did to her. His imagination went wild thinking about all the things he and Rio had yet to do to her.

God, she responded to their every touch. Her ex had obviously never tapped into her wild passion. Now that she had experienced it, she would crave it. He vowed that only he and Rio would satisfy her.

Their passions had been denied for years and would now be turned loose on Jesse. He looked up to see Rio watching Jesse in fascination. He must have felt Clay's eyes on him because he looked up, meeting his brother's gaze.

The hunger in Rio's eyes no doubt reflected in his own. "She's ours," Rio breathed so only Clay could hear.

Clay nodded and they both looked back at the woman over his lap, the woman they both had already fallen more than half in love with. They had tapped her passionate nature and would continue to explore it, and her, thoroughly.

Clay stroked his fingers in and out of her ass marveling at how tightly she gripped them. Her moans filled the room.

"Your ass is so tight, baby." Clay knew by the way her muscles clenched that her orgasm loomed close. He wanted his mouth on her smooth pussy when she came.

Pulling his fingers from her, he grabbed one of the anal plugs they had gotten today. Knowing that they had almost no control with Jesse, they had already brought their purchases home and readied them for tonight.

Seeing the look on Rio's face, Clay handed the plug to him. They grinned at each other when Jesse squirmed.

"Please, I want to come." Jesse panted and tried to push off Clay's thighs.

She moaned, then gasped when Rio positioned the plug against her anus.

"Easy darlin'" Rio crooned to her. "Relax those muscles so I can push this plug into your bottom."

Clay felt the shivers that went through Jesse as Rio pressed the plug into her.

"Oh, God!" Jesse's moan thrilled him as Clay watched the plug disappear into her ass. He felt her shiver and wasted no time, lifting her and laying her back on the bed, positioning her legs as they hung over the side.

Clay knelt between her thighs, lifting them.

"Now I get to lap up this pussy. Come for us, baby." Clay lowered his head and sucked her clit into his mouth.

Jesse screamed as her orgasm hit her, shaking uncontrollably. She arched and shook, her limbs jerking so hard that she inadvertently dislodged Clay's mouth.

"Uh, uh, baby." He pulled her back, firmly holding her thighs in his grip. "I'm not done yet."

Rio lay naked and aroused next to her. Clay heard him murmuring praises to her and looked up to see his brother brushing the hair from Jesse's face.

"You're beautiful, darlin'." Rio's mouth covered hers as Clay's pushed his tongue into her pussy.

"Oh, baby, you taste so good." Clay breathed and resumed lapping her juices, sliding his tongue from her pussy to her clit and back again.

"Told ya," Rio lifted his head and glanced at his brother before turning his fierce gaze back to her. "And she's all ours. I'm going to enjoy eating that pussy every day."

"I want to be inside this soft pussy when you come, baby. Turn over and take Rio into your mouth."

He flipped her effortlessly onto her stomach, pulling her to her knees and positioned her the way he wanted.

"Just imagine what it's going to feel like when we get our cocks inside that tight ass." Clay pushed on the plug and twisted it.

"Oh my God!" Jesse sobbed.

Rio lifted her until she rested on his thighs as he lay back. He stroked his length with one hand, cupping the back of her head with the other.

"Come on, darlin'. Let me feel that hot mouth on my cock. I've been thinking about my cock in that mouth of yours all day."

Clay watched his brother's face and knew when Jesse took him in her mouth. He heard Rio hiss then groan.

Clay watched his brother with their woman, his love for her growing.

"Told ya." He threw his brother's words back at him and grinned as Rio's features tightened with the strain of holding off his orgasm.

"Let's see how tight this pussy is with your ass plugged, baby." Clay positioned the head of his cock at her pussy entrance and pushed his hips forward.

Jesse moaned as Clay entered her, the vibration making Rio hiss again.

Clay wanted to laugh, but with the feel of Jesse's hot silky pussy quivering as she stretched to accept him, he managed only a choked moan.

Jesse's determination to make both men lose control faltered, as thoughts left her, leaving only the ability to feel. She no longer thought of trying to drive Rio quickly to release with her mouth. She only knew she craved his taste and used her mouth on him ruthlessly, trying to take him as deep as she could into her throat. She wanted to explore every bump and ridge, to know the feel of him on her tongue, needing to know him as intimately as possible.

She didn't think about making Clay lose control. She wanted to feel his cock hard and deep inside her forever. She felt so full that it bordered on pain but she didn't want this feeling to ever end.

Both men voiced their pleasure. Their praises and moans intoxicated her, driving her higher.

She felt her orgasm approaching as Rio stiffened, roaring as he came, hot jets of his seed hitting the back of her throat. She swallowed furiously, her orgasm fast approaching. She released his cock as she came, screaming as the contractions tightened her pussy and anus.

The burn of it, the too tight feeling sent her immediately into another, even more explosive orgasm that took her breath as she dig her fingers into Rio's thighs. She heard Clay groan as he tunneled deep inside her, his hands on her hips hard when his cock pulsed as his come shot to her womb.

For several long minutes, no one moved. Heavy breathing and groans filled the room as all three of them tried to recover from the intensity of what had just happened.

Eventually she felt Clay slide from her pussy and his lips on her neck as he nuzzled her, his breathing still ragged. He moved to lie beside her and stroked her back as Rio stroked her hair. She liked this part almost as much as the sex.

Jesse's eyes remained closed. A deep sense of contentment filled her as she felt Clay and Rio's touch. Exhausted from the demands they had made of her, she'd never felt so completely sated in her life.

"We need a shower," Rio groaned tiredly to no one in particular.

"Never moving again," Jesse slurred against his chest.

She felt his chuckle as his chest rumbled beneath her. She smiled and nuzzled him as she sought a more comfortable position.

Clay sat up and lightly slapped her bottom.

"Come on, baby. You'll sleep better when you've had a shower."

Jesse jumped when she felt the slap, lifting her head and reaching down to rub her still warm rear.

"I have to go take the plug out first."

"No, baby." Clay lifted her off Rio's chest to carry her into the bathroom.

"Damn it!"

Clay laughed at his brother's protest, moving with their exhausted lover into the bathroom. He anxious anticipated moving into the house next door with the much bigger shower.

"What do you mean, no?" Jesse lifted her head from his shoulder. "I want to take it out."

"It's better if you leave it in for now." Clay bent his head and kissed her forehead as he stepped into the shower with her. "We need to stretch you so that you can take us both."

She looked so small and adorable as she looked up at him through her lashes.

"It's going to hurt, isn't it? You're too big for both of you to fit."

Clay couldn't prevent the big grin that crossed his face. She looked so cute.

"That's why we need to stretch that tight little ass of yours." He poured shampoo into his hand and began lathering her hair.

"Don't worry, baby. Rio and I are gonna make it so good for you that you'll want us in your pussy and ass together all the time. Which is good because that's where we'll be."

She didn't look convinced but her protests stopped. He washed her thoroughly, soaping her newly waxed pussy carefully.

He reluctantly handed her off to Rio to dry while he hurriedly finished his own shower so he could get back to her. He wanted to hold her close and cuddle a little before they slept.

Idly he wondered if he should be surprised by how vital she had already become to both of them.

Chapter 7

Jesse woke the next morning curled around Clay.

"Good morning, baby." He rolled her until she lay over him, tilting her face for his kiss. Heat pooled low in her stomach. His hands on her hips sent little tingles up her spine. The plug shifted, bringing back memories of the night before.

When she felt his hard arousal against her stomach, she experienced a heady feeling of feminine power.

It aroused her and made her playful, the feeling so foreign it briefly disconcerted her. She forgot it though when she looked in his eyes. The heat there nearly took her breath away.

"Good morning, handsome," she murmured against his lips and was rewarded with a cocky grin.

His cock jumped as she straddled his hips.

"It looks like you're awake."

"Oh, baby, I'm *very* awake."

Jesse reached down and wrapped her hands around his thick length, smiling when he groaned and hardened even more.

"You look happy to see me." Jesse lowered her eyes and looked at him coquettishly, noting the glimpse of surprise and pleasure in his eyes as she teased him.

Rio came out of the bathroom with a towel wrapped around his waist, grinning when he saw her.

"It looks like our little darlin' is awake."

"I'm *very* awake."

Clay roared with laughter while Rio looked at the two of them in confusion.

Clay's laughter ended with a choked breath when Jesse lifted up and lowered herself onto his cock.

"Jesus, Jesse!" Clay grasped her hips, steadying her as she sank onto his length.

With the plug still snug inside her ass, his cock felt huge as he filled her.

Jesse established a slow rhythm, teasing them both. Rio moved to kneel on the bed beside them, bending to take her mouth with his.

Fire raced through her. Rio's mouth moved on hers, matching her playful mood as he teased her with his lips and tongue, smiling against her mouth as she grasped his hair in her fists in demand.

He reached for her hands and placed them on Clay's hard thighs behind her, pushing the anal plug further into her. The position left her wide open for them, her breasts thrust out, her hands behind her. She couldn't move them as they held her up and Rio, the devil, made sure she stayed leaning back just enough to need her hands to support herself.

Rio tweaked her nipples and watched her as though fascinated.

She tried to move, to thrust herself faster on Clay's cock, but he held her hips easily, keeping the rhythm slow and steady.

"Faster! Harder!"

"You wanted to tease me, baby. I'm just giving you a taste of your own medicine."

She felt his cock push slowly deep inside her, touching her womb before lifting her until only the large head remained inside her. She tried to force his cock back inside her hard and fast, but he only chuckled as he lowered her inch by agonizing inch down until he was once more seated to the hilt.

She felt Rio's hand slide from her breast to her stomach and continue lower. She drew a harsh breath and groaned when the heat from his hand moved over her clit. She panted and struggled as Clay lifted her again and slammed into her forcefully at the same time Rio pinched her clit.

She screamed as she came with Clay continuing his forceful thrusts, her clit pulsing as Rio continued to stroke it, layering one orgasm over the other.

Clay roared as he came and her arms buckled. Rio caught her around her shoulders and slowed his strokes, gradually bringing her down.

Clay pulled her forward until she sprawled bonelessly across his chest and soothingly stroked her back.

She felt his lips on her hair and sighed contentedly. She felt Rio move and realized that he hadn't come yet. Opening one eye, she saw that he had a very impressive erection, his cock pointing toward his flat stomach.

"Rio?" Jesse started to get up, surprised when Clay's arms tightened around her. She looked up at him in confusion.

"But, Rio…"

"Don't worry, baby. You're going to take good care of Rio."

She jerked when she felt Rio separate the cheeks of her ass and grab the base of the plug.

"I'm taking this one out, darlin'."

Clay held her still as Rio removed the plug, pulling her face down for a lingering kiss.

"Go take your shower, baby. I'll get your coffee."

Rio hauled her off his brother, pulling her roughly against his chest. He lowered his face to hers as she pulled his hair in her fists, kissing him hungrily as she reached for his cock.

"Uh, uh, darlin'" He grabbed her hands in his and held them to his chest. "After you take your shower, I'm gonna push the bigger plug into that tight ass and fuck that tight pussy long and hard."

With one last burning kiss, he turned her and swatted her bottom. "Move!"

Jesse giggled and floated toward the bathroom. She closed the door and seeing herself in the mirror, froze.

Was that her?

She glowed! Looking closely at herself, she couldn't believe the gold sparkle in her eyes and the stupid grin she couldn't quite manage to wipe off her face.

Shaking her head she headed for the shower, anxious to get back to Rio.

* * * *

Returning to the bedroom wearing only a towel, her empty coffee cup in her hand, she smiled.

Rio stood next to the bed gloriously naked, his hard angry looking cock demanding her attention.

Clay lounged on the bed, sipping coffee from a thick mug as he watched her approach, his eyes full of amusement. His dark hair looked damp. He must have taken a shower in the other bathroom while she'd taken hers.

She moved toward Rio, her nipples already hard, her pussy already damp in anticipation. A few days ago she would have been surprised but she had already begun to get used to her body's response to these two men.

She reached up on her toes for Rio's kiss, her hands moving up his chest. She felt her towel drop and knew that Clay watched, adding another layer to her arousal.

Breaking away from Rio's mouth, she started to kneel, needing to taste him.

He stopped her downward move with a tug and turned her toward the bed.

"Not this time, sugar." His voice sounded gravelly. "I'm too far gone."

He bent her over the edge of the bed, tugging a pillow under her hips. "Thinking of pushing that larger plug into your ass and fucking that tight pussy has my control a little shaky."

Jesse felt a heady sense of power at his admission. To think that she could make a man such as this one lose control, even a little, because of his desire for her thrilled her.

Clay moved to her, claiming her lips in a kiss so dark and deep, it had her heart galloping. He shifted back to trail a finger down her cheek.

"You're beautiful, baby."

"Oh, darlin', when I finally get my cock in this tight ass, I'm gonna fuck you so hard and deep that neither of us may survive it."

Clay smiled at her. "Yeah, the same thought has crossed my mind a time or two," he told his brother, his eyes never leaving Jesse's.

"Imagine how it's going to feel when we're both deep inside her."

Clay reached under her to tease a nipple as Rio lubed her. She shivered as the plug pressed against her tight entrance and moved passed the tight ring of muscle.

It burned even as it pleasured, her body unconsciously grasping the plug.

"I can't," she panted even as her body craved the burn.

"Relax, baby." Clay reached for her clit, his touch light and coaxing. "Let Rio stretch you a little more."

With Rio stroking the plug steadily in and out of her, gaining ground with each stroke and Clay's hands on her breasts and clit, Jesse felt herself loosening more and more, allowing Rio to push the plug deeper and deeper inside her.

She felt herself opening to his insistent slow thrusts, her back arching as she reveled in the sensations.

"That's it darlin'." Rio praised her as he pushed the plug all the way inside her.

Jesse felt Rio's tongue slide into her pussy and her toes curled. He flipped her over onto her back and dove for her again, his tongue relentless as he explored her bare folds. She felt the signs of her impending orgasm.

Her pussy felt so sensitive, especially now that it had been waxed. Clay and Rio seemed to love it bare and spent a great deal of time learning how she responded to every touch. They explored her body, finding all her weaknesses and appeared to take great satisfaction of her vulnerability as they used their knowledge ruthlessly.

It almost frightened her to see how quickly they made her body respond to them.

Rio's mouth drove her to her first orgasm so quickly it took her breath. Clay held Jesse's wrists high over her head in one strong hand as he murmured in her ear.

"Rio's enjoying lapping up all your sweet juices. Now that you're waxed and staying that way, you can't hide from us. Everything is bare and soft."

Rio pushed his tongue inside her, placing her feet on his shoulders to open her even further. Clay's mouth moved to the closest nipple while he pinched the other.

When Rio grasped the plug and twisted, she arched helplessly, trying to pull her hands free from Clay's grasp.

Clay held her firmly. To her surprise, this heightened her arousal and she moaned. She knew Clay realized her reaction to his firm hold when he chuckled.

"Your hands are staying right where they are." His grin was lethal. "We like you helpless while we have our way with you. Besides, your breasts stand up so beautifully when your hands are like this, as if they're begging for my attention." He flicked a tongue over her nipple, causing her to gasp. "And look how sensitive they are."

Her head tossed back and forth on the bed as Rio's mouth moved to her clit. Oh, she was so close!

She could have wept when he lifted his head.

"I've got to fuck you, darlin'" He stood and positioned his cock at her pussy entrance and thrust his length to the hilt.

Jesse screamed as her body fought to accommodate him. She felt her inner muscles ripple as she tried to accept the almost overwhelming fullness.

"Fuck!" Rio's features appeared carved from granite as he struggled to remain still.

* * * *

Rio could feel Jesse's body struggle to accommodate him. Feeling the muscles in her pussy quiver as she tried to adapt to his cock gave him more pleasure than he could ever remember.

Never had anything ever felt this good. He wanted nothing more than to fuck her, ruthlessly hammer into her over and over until they both exploded.

But he knew moving before her body adjusted would hurt her and he wouldn't do that for anything in the world.

He watched as Jesse's eyes squeezed shut. "Oh, it's too good." His cock jumped at her tortured cry.

"Fuck me, damn it!" She tilted her hips and he hissed, his body shaking with the strain of remaining still.

"Stay still, darlin'. I don't want to hurt you."

Her hips pumped as she tried to get him to move. "I'm not made of glass. If you don't move, I'm going to scream!"

"You're going to scream anyway, sugar."

She became so wild in her passion that he was having trouble holding onto her.

"Are you going to fuck me or talk me to death? If you're afraid to take me, move so Clay can do it."

Rio's eyes narrowed even as his cock jumped at the challenge. What could a man do when his woman challenged him like that?

He saw the surprise on Clay's face even as he pulled his cock almost completely out of her and plunged forcefully deep inside her tight, hot pussy, the fire in his blood ignited by his lover's demands.

Jesse felt the force of Rio's thrusts shift the plug. She felt so full. Her eyes stayed on Rio as his thrusts became more and more urgent.

Satisfaction spread through her when his control finally snapped. She could see it in the wildness in his eyes as he pounded into her.

Between one thrust and the next she came. She arched as Rio slammed deep inside her one last time, her orgasm triggering his.

She couldn't move even when Clay released her hands and smoothed his over her trembling body. Rio collapsed next to her, his soothing touch joining his brother's as they slowly brought her back to earth.

Once again she lay nestled warmly between her two lovers as they calmed her with their hands and lips, making her feel safe and warm and wanted.

She had grown to love this time after sex as much as she enjoyed the sex itself.

Just as she had grown to love both of them.

Chapter 8

Jesse's mind raced with possibilities. She and Kelly could begin some of their new ideas here. This place had plenty of room for their workroom and for storage.

The two large front rooms would be their showroom. Once they took the dark drapes down and washed the windows light would fill the room.

"Do you think Kelly will move here?" Nat asked as she continued her perusal of one of the front rooms.

The meeting with the leasing agent had gone better than expected and Jesse already had the keys. She wouldn't sign the lease until she talked to Kelly. Once she had explained the situation, the owner had agreed to give her the keys when she paid the first month's rent.

"I hope so." Jesse sighed. "I'll call her later when Clay and Rio are still busy on the ranch. It's too early to call her now. She'll be busy with the bottling and would be distracted."

"Why won't you tell Clay and Rio what you're doing? They'll be thrilled."

"I don't want Clay and Rio to know anything about this yet." When Nat started to speak, Jesse held up a hand to silence her. "First, I have to find out if Kelly even wants to move here. I think she will, but I don't know for sure."

"So if Kelly says yes, you'll tell them?"

"Eventually." Jesse sighed again. "Look Nat, for them this could be only sex."

Nat frowned. "But, Jesse…"

"Nat, the three of us just started this," she waved her hand in the air, "whatever it is. We haven't known each other very long, certainly not long enough to talk about a future. They went into this thinking that I came here only for a short visit. Our relationship, or whatever it is, began with the three of us thinking that. I don't want them to think that I'm moving here to pressure them into something that they don't want. They'll think I'm pushy and taking a lot for granted if they thought that I moved here expecting something from them."

"I don't think they will think anything like that, Jesse. You need to tell them." Jesse felt Nat touch her shoulder. "I really think that Clay and Rio want you to stay. Please tell them, Jesse."

"Not yet, Nat. And remember your promise. You are not to tell anyone yet, okay?"

Nat blew out a frustrated breath. She had also promised her husband that she wouldn't repeat the conversation she had overheard when Clay and Rio ordered an engagement ring and wedding bands for Jesse. Both men appeared to be flat out crazy for her and seemed confident that she was the one that they had been waiting for.

"Yes," Nat agreed reluctantly. "I remember my promise, Jesse. I won't say a word to anyone." Everything seemed to be falling into place for three of her very good friends, even if they didn't realize it yet.

When Jesse's cell phone rang, she grinned. "It's Alex."

Rifling through her purse, she found it.

"Hello, sweetheart. How are you?"

Nat watched Jesse's face crumble.

"Is Alex alright?"

Jesse patted Nat's arm reassuringly and frowned.

"Why are you calling me, Brian, and from Alex's cell phone?"

"The reason that you didn't have my cell number is because I didn't want you to have it. You have the other numbers, although I wish you'd stop using them. We have nothing to talk about." Nat watched Jesse rub her forehead.

"You're visiting Alex? Why? So you could get my number? Where is he? So, you used his phone to find me while he's taking a shower. What's so important?"

Nat paced back and forth across the windows as she watched Jesse listen to whatever her ex husband had to say. The frown on Jesse's face told her it couldn't be good.

"It's really none of your business what I'm doing in Oklahoma. No, I'm not sending you any money! If you would stop conning people out of their money, you wouldn't have to worry about things like that."

Nat wondered if Brian heard the change in Jesse. She sounded angry and animated as she talked to him, a far cry from the woman she had met at the airport. Her relationship with Clay and Rio had brought her back to life.

"Nothing is wrong with me, Brian, except that I don't want to talk to you and I want you to leave Alex out of your problems.

"No, I don't have a lover. I have two!"

Jesse snapped the phone shut with a grimace.

"Are you okay, honey?"

Jesse sighed. "Yeah. He just makes me so mad. He never paid any attention to me when we were married, except to ask for money. Now that we're divorced, he thinks he can still ask me for money and ask about my private life."

Jesse rubbed her forehead. "I've got to talk to Kelly today and make a decision about what we're going to do. Then, I've got to tell Brian, or he'll hound Alex to find me. If he's pissed someone off by cheating them out of their money, I don't want him anywhere near Alex."

Nat watched Jesse pace and could see the headache forming in her eyes.

"Do you think he'll show up here looking for money?" Nat thought about how much money Clay and Rio had and knew Jesse didn't know. But if Brian learned it, he would pay Jesse a visit.

"I doubt it." She turned away. "He wouldn't want to go to the trouble of coming here."

* * * *

"Thanks, Jake. I appreciate the call."

"Damn it!" Clay slammed his cell phone shut, barely resisting the urge to throw it.

"What is it?" Rio turned from where he had been leaning on the fence watching the horses being exercised.

"Jake called. Evidently Jesse was with Nat today. Nat told Jake that Brian went to see Alex when he couldn't reach Jesse at home." When Rio lifted a brow, Clay continued. "Brian didn't have Jesse's cell number but knew that Alex does. He called Jesse from Alex's phone wanting money. Jake thinks someone is trying to recoup some money Brian conned him out of."

"Shit, why didn't she say something when she got back?" Rio shouted and glared at the house with Jesse inside.

"I don't know, but I'm going to find out." He stormed toward the house aware of Rio striding angrily behind him. "Jake said that Nat's really upset. He's sure she's not telling him everything, which he plans to remedy. But she did tell him that Jesse had a terrible headache after talking to him. He also said that Jesse told her ex about us." Satisfaction went through him as he thought about her admission that there was an *us*.

"Did she tell him that we would be more than happy to kick his ass if he showed up here with any thoughts of bothering her?"

"It seems we have a few things to discuss with our woman." Clay strode determinedly toward the house pausing when he heard Jesse's voice through the back door.

"Oh, honey, I found a wonderful place for us."

Clay exchanged glances with his brother, who'd stopped next to him.

"You're going to love this place. We can fix it up and do a lot of the things we talked about."

Clay's stomach knotted. She couldn't be talking to her ex husband, could she?

"Don't worry about it. He knows where you are now. If you come out here, he wouldn't be able to find you, at least for a while." She laughed. "Clay and Rio would hurt him if I asked them to. They're crazy about me. I'll turn them loose on him. They'll do anything for me."

Clay raised a brow at that.

"No, I haven't told them yet. I already told you that I'll tell them when the time is right. Don't worry about what's going on between me and them. I'll deal with them in my own way."

"She'll deal with us?" Rio mouthed.

"So, honey, are you moving out here with me or not? I have to sign the lease as soon as possible. Yes, of course I'm happy. I have everything I could possibly want. Will you be able to pack everything? Okay. Could you get my clothes and stuff from the house? I'll call the realtor and arrange to sell everything else. I want a brand new start."

Clay wiped a hand over his face and looked at his brother. Rio looked as if he'd been kicked in the stomach.

"I love you, too. Call me when you're on your way. Bye."

Both men watched through the window as Jesse did a little happy dance in the middle of their kitchen.

Not being able to stand it anymore, Clay cursed and strode away, Rio close behind. Reaching the barn, Clay surprised them both by slamming his fist through the wall.

"That lying bitch!"

Rio looked at the hole his brother had made. Clay had always been the cool one, the one always in control. His brother's surge of anger seemed so out of character that it startled him. He couldn't stand to see the terrible rage and pain that glittered in his brother's eyes.

His own eyes burned. The way Jesse had opened up and responded to them had led them to believe that she truly felt something for them. For the first time in his life he had begun to believe, really believe that they could finally have the life they'd always wanted.

Now it was over.

"She lied about everything," Rio croaked, the lump in his throat threatening to choke him.

He braced his arms against the barn wall, hanging his head in anguish.

When Clay turned, his features appeared to be carved in stone. "I don't want her to know how much she's hurt us. You stay here. I'll go end this."

Rio straightened and turned, wiping all expression from his face.

"No." He paused to swallow the lump in his throat. "We're in this together."

* * * *

Waiting for Clay and Rio in the living room, Jesse could hardly contain her excitement. Kelly sounded excited about starting over and relieved when Jesse assured her that she would be free of Simon.

She would try to tell Clay and Rio tonight. She wanted to work her way around it, try to broach the subject matter-of-factly so they wouldn't feel pressured.

When she heard the back screen slam shut, her heart raced. Her nipples hardened when she heard their footsteps. She had seen them briefly after coming back from town, only an hour ago? It seemed like much longer.

They wanted to spend some time watching the new men they had hired. They didn't say it but she knew they did it so they could spend more time with her.

She didn't make demands on their time, but they all enjoyed spending as much time together as possible. Greedy for each other, they carved out as much time as they could together.

Her pussy dampened when they entered the room. They were big and strong and, at least for now, all hers.

Her welcoming smiled faltered when she saw their faces.

"Is something wrong?"

"Why should anything be wrong?" Clay's usually tender face, at least when he looked at her, lacked all emotion. "Unless there's something you want to tell us?"

Jesse's stomach tightened. They had already found out. Did they know the leasing agent, or had they heard it from someone he had told?

That's what she got for trying to keep a secret in a small town.

"I'd planned to tell you tonight." She touched Clay's sleeve and felt the blood drain from her face when he shrugged her off.

Tears pricked her lids and she blinked rapidly to get rid of them. They certainly didn't look happy that she planned to move here. She'd hoped she was wrong, but what they'd had had been a fling. Apparently she meant nothing more to them than that.

She'd really begun to believe that they had begun to build something wonderful together.

"It doesn't matter," Clay said, dismissing her easily. "Rio and I had a good time with you, but you really didn't think it was anything more than just sex, did you?" His words and the amusement on his face ripped her to shreds.

Stupid! Stupid! Stupid! She knew better than to let herself feel.

She felt the cool mask slip into place with the ease of years of practice. Jesse could feel the withdrawal into herself, barriers erecting but too late to stop the pain.

"I guess I should be leaving." Her eyes caressed her lovers' faces once more.

"I think that would be best." Rio spoke for the first time, his eyes as she'd never seen them, hard and cold.

Jesse nodded, not trusting herself to speak and turned to walk away.

"Don't bother calling us for help if trouble follows. You're no longer under our protection."

Jesse felt the knife slice right through her heart. She couldn't believe after what they'd shared, that they cared so little for her. Nothing. She meant nothing to them.

Walking down the deserted road towards town, Jesse let the tears fall freely down her face as she promised herself, *never again!*

Jesse called Nat from her cell phone and had her tears dried before Nat got to her.

"What happened, honey?"

"Please take me to the shop. I'm going to move into the apartment upstairs. Could you ask Jake if he would mind picking up my suitcase? I left without it."

"What happened, Jesse?"

Jesse sighed and let her head drop onto the headrest. "They found out about the shop." She shook her head when Nat started to speak. "No, I don't think you told them. They must have found out from the agent or someone he told. It's a small town, Nat."

"They weren't happy about it?" Nat frowned.

"No, apparently not. They told me that they had wanted only sex. They also told me not to call them if trouble followed me here. I'm no longer under their protection. Hell, I've been protecting myself long enough. I don't need them to protect me."

She turned to Nat. "How do you think they found out that someone's after Brian for money?"

Nat grimaced. "From Jake. I'm sorry, Jesse. I told Jake that Brian called you and that it upset you that he tried to get money from you."

"Well if Brian, or anyone else," she thought briefly of Simon. "shows up, I'll take care of it just like I always have. I don't need some man to take care of me."

Nat reached over and grasped Jesse's hand. "Does that mean you're still going to move here?"

Jesse thought about the empty life she had back in Maryland. Thought about Kelly's life. The business they worked hard on.

Clay and Rio's faces as they loved her, no, fucked her, swam through her mind almost making her give into the urge to turn tail and run.

But, Kelly had been so excited. Nat lived here and she had missed her sister terribly. Jesse loved the town, a town that Kelly and the business would thrive in. She needed the money from the business not only to support herself, but to help Alex with his expenses at school. Besides, just because Clay and Rio didn't want her anymore she saw no reason to stay away from her sister.

"Yes." Jesse nodded, determined. "I'm staying."

Chapter 10

Several hours later Jake dropped off her suitcases. Nat had told him about Jesse's store since the reason for keeping it a secret it from him no longer existed. He smiled when he remembered her face when he warned her that he would be taking care of her punishment for keeping something from him.

He would have to do something a little unexpected, a little harsh so that she wouldn't be so cocky the next time. He had to do something that would make his headstrong wife think twice before keeping secrets from him again.

He looked at Jesse and couldn't prevent the rush of anger at what his friends had done. They wouldn't even talk about it.

"Rio called and asked me if I would bring these to you," he told her now.

"Thanks Jake, I appreciate it."

Jake winced inwardly when he saw that her eyes looked dead again, devoid of all emotion as she looked at him.

He wanted to hit something, preferably two hard headed idiots he called friends. Jesse looked devastated, but trying hard not to show it. He had learned how to read women and this one built walls around her so solidly that he could almost see them.

Her features appeared to be carefully schooled before turning away from his scrutiny to resume the task of readying her apartment.

Had it been only yesterday that he'd seen her face glow, her eyes full of love and laughter as she looked at Clay and Rio?

"I don't know what to say to you, Jesse." He ran a hand through his hair in frustration. "I've known them a long time and I've never seen either of them react to any woman the way they did with you. I don't understand what happened between you that made them turn their backs on you this way."

"Don't worry about it, Jake." Jesse shook her head. "They didn't make any promises. They never lied to me. It was a fling. No big deal."

"No big deal? But they…" Jake snapped his mouth shut as he thought about the rings they had ordered for her.

"They what?"

"They're idiots and I'm going to knock their heads together!"

Jesse spun around. "No! Promise me you won't say anything to them. Just because Nat wanted it to work out doesn't mean that you have to get involved. They don't want me anymore. I'm fine with that. Promise me you won't interfere."

"Okay, honey. I won't interfere if you promise me something."

"What?" Jesse asked warily.

"I want your promise that if Brian or Simon or anyone that comes trying to get money from you that your ex conned from them shows up, that you'll call me right away. Do you promise?"

"Jake, I can take care of—"

"Then I guess I'll go have a nice long talk with Clay and Rio."

"Damn it, Jake!"

"Do you promise to call me?"

"I promise," Jesse sighed.

"Good. Give me your cell phone."

Jake programmed his number into Jesse's phone, aware that she watched.

He handed the phone back to her. "Any time, day or night. I'm also going to talk to the sheriff and a few others." He raised a hand to silence her when she would have protested. "I'll make sure no one says anything to Clay or Rio about this, but there's no way I'm going to allow anyone to hurt either you or your friend Kelly."

He felt his stomach churn when Jesse just nodded and turned away.

* * * *

Jesse woke smiling and stretched, wondering what Clay and Rio had planned for her today. Opening her eyes she couldn't prevent the sob from escaping as she suddenly remembered.

She wasn't in a big warm bed snuggled next to her lovers. She lay on a cot in her and Kelly's new apartment.

Angry that she felt sorry for herself, she jumped up and started the coffee before heading for the shower.

Kelly would be arriving some time today. Her call last night had spurred Jesse into action. She'd finished cleaning the apartment and the store so when Kelly and her brother arrived in the moving truck with all of her and Kelly's belongings everything would be ready.

Kelly wanted to bring most of her own furniture. Jesse had arranged to have all of hers sold.

Stepping into the shower, she grimaced and rubbed a hand over her lower back. She would have to buy a bed. The one time she had tried to shop for one, she couldn't prevent imagining Clay and Rio in it with her.

She had immediately turned and walked out of the store and had yet to find the courage to go back.

The cot would do for now.

Kelly and her brother Cullen arrived early in the afternoon. Kelly hopped from the truck and raced over to Jesse. Jesse barely had time to brace herself before Kelly launched herself at her.

"Thank you, Jesse. Thanks for not leaving me behind."

Jesse squeezed her friend who looked more her age than she had since Jesse had known her. The stress that made her look much older than her twenty four years had been replaced by a glowing smile and flushed cheeks, her eyes clear of the fatigue that always showed in them.

Jesse could see the excitement on her friend's face. "Go on Kelly. Have a look. See if you like it."

"Go ahead." Cullen smiled indulgently at his sister as he joined them on the sidewalk. "I'm going to get everything ready to unload. You two need to figure out where you want everything."

When Jesse moved to follow Kelly, Cullen stopped her with a hand on her arm.

"Wait a minute."

Jesse looked up at him, watching as he waited for Kelly to enter the building before turning to her.

"I want to thank you for what you do for my sister."

When he smiled at her she noted absently that he'd become even more handsome than the last time she saw him. She knew he always had the women panting after him and it was only a matter of time before one caught him.

"I love Kelly." Jesse glanced at the building and smiled when she heard Kelly exclaim over something. "We went through a lot together because of Brian and Simon. She's like a little sister to me."

He pushed a stray lock of hair behind her ear. "I know how you've put yourself between Kelly and Simon. I know you've been hurt. It scares me."

He raised a hand when she would have spoken.

"While I stayed with her, I tried to talk Kelly into moving to Virginia with me, but she won't. She wants her independence and she loves your business partnership. She feels good with you. After your call, this was all she talked about. She loves you, too. So do I."

He grasped her arms. "I want you to promise me that if either of you need anything, you'll call me. And if this town doesn't turn out to be what you think it is, both of you are always welcome to come live with me."

"Thanks, Cullen. We'll be fine."

"It's good to know that you'll be looked after. Where are these two men that I've been hearing so much about?"

"That was only temporary." She shrugged and turned away, only to be turned back.

Cullen's gaze sharpened. "That's not what Kelly said. She's been so happy for you. What happened? Do I need to kick their asses?"

Jesse couldn't prevent the bubble of laughter that spilled out. Cullen was big, easily over six feet, leanly muscled and in his prime. But the thought of him kicking Clay or Rio's ass made her laugh.

"No, but thanks." She started to turn away but Cullen stopped her.

"I can never thank you enough for what you do for Kelly." He bent to kiss her cheek. "Thanks, Jesse."

"There is something you can do for me." Jesse saw Jake and Blade approaching.

"What is it, Jesse?"

"Unload the truck." Laughing at Cullen's surprised grin, she introduced him to the other men and headed into the store to find Kelly.

* * * *

Jesse and Kelly spent the next week moving into the apartment, doing the paperwork necessary for the store and making and bottling new products. Their full days left them exhausted, but Jesse lay in her cot at night missing Clay and Rio's warmth surrounding her.

Her nipples hardened and her pussy wept with the need to be with them, to have them deep inside her, touching her in a way no one else ever had. She had never even gotten to experience both of them loving her at the same time and now she never would.

She wept with the need to have them near, their presence making her feel wanted, feminine, secure. She missed their voices, their scents, their laughter.

Kelly and Nat commented more than once on her appearance as the sleepless night continued. She had shadows under her puffy eyes that got darker every day. She grew more and more tired and listless.

Cullen stayed long enough to help them move in and get settled before returning to Virginia. Since then Kelly and Jesse spent their time not only getting the store ready, but also exploring their new home.

Everyone welcomed them and the women seemed anxious to try their products. Their enthusiasm excited Kelly even more but Jesse couldn't seem to summon the energy for it.

She tried to put on a good front but the way Kelly, Nat and even Jake looked at her, she could tell they saw right through it.

Jesse didn't see Clay or Rio. When she realized it, the pain in her heart nearly undid her. Living in a town as small as Desire, normally you could count on running into almost everyone within a few days. Not to have seen them at all meant that they had to be purposely avoiding her.

She didn't expect anything from them after their brief affair. She'd left when they'd asked her to, hadn't she? She hadn't bothered them at all and yet they avoided her as though she had somehow wronged them.

Why? Just because she'd stayed?

Thinking about that and missing them despite how they obviously felt about her kept her awake at night.

Another thing that kept her awake at night was Brian.

She'd told him that she'd moved here so he wouldn't bother Alex. He had an irritating habit of showing up unexpectedly with his hand out.

Now that he had her cell number, he kept calling. At first he asked for money, then pleaded. When she continued to say no, his calls became increasingly demanding, then furious.

The stress of dealing with these calls exhausted her as did trying to keep it from both Nat and Kelly. She could handle Brian. She had for years. She certainly didn't need either of them to tell Jake, who'd started watching her like a hawk.

Jesse leaned against the window and sighed, closing her eyes as weariness washed over her, suddenly overwhelmed at always having to be strong. She wanted to lay her head on a strong shoulder, be held securely in strong arms and told that everything would be okay.

Already they'd weakened her.

Lying in her cot at night, tears flowed freely down her face as she wept silently in the dark. Immersed in fatigue, she longed for the heartache to stop.

Putting those walls back up between her and the rest of the world seemed harder than it had ever been before.

Putting up those walls to protect her from being hurt as Clay and Rio continued to avoid her seemed to be impossible.

Chapter 10

Clay fisted his hand and smashed it down hard on the smooth granite countertop. The house that he and his brother had built while waiting for the woman of their dreams was complete.

His gaze took in the warm colors, new appliances and yards of counter space. When building the house he'd imagined it filled with the love and laughter he and his brother had grown up with.

He could clearly remember both of their fathers' laughter and their mother's giggles. Their dads had constantly touched their mother, stealing kisses while she made dinner, playing with her hair as they sat together watching television and always pulling her down onto one of their laps for a cuddle.

He wanted that kind of relationship. As they'd worked on the house, he'd considered it all a labor of love for the faceless woman they waited for.

Now as he looked around the kitchen, he thought of twinkling brown eyes and a saucy smile being wiped out and replaced with hurt. He'd wanted to shake her when that cold, emotionless look had slipped into place and her eyes had become flat.

The only woman he could imagine here now had a face and a name.

Jesse.

"I don't get it." Rio took a hearty swallow of his beer. He and Clay had been working their asses off at the ranch for a week, hoping the physical exertion would wear them out so they could sleep without thinking about Jesse.

So far it hadn't worked.

Tonight they decided to get away from the ranch so they had come into town for a beer. They'd talked about going to the club and decided that neither of them could even imagine going there yet. They didn't want to watch their single friends enjoying sex with one of the women who frequented the place for just that reason.

They had absolutely no desire to fuck any of the women there. They craved a woman who always smelled of peaches combined with her own unique scent.

They certainly couldn't stand to hear the conversations of their married friends who talked about their beloved wives. They would be reminded just how much they had lost when they lost Jesse.

Their faint hope had disappeared and they had pretty much resigned themselves to never finding the woman they needed.

The thought of just grabbing Jesse and bringing her back to the ranch had crossed their minds a few times. Probably the wrong thing to do and still…

So they sat nursing their beers in The Bar. Their friends John and Michael, who owned the place, saw no reason to call it anything but that.

"Why is everyone looking at us like we kicked their puppy?" Rio mused, glancing around the bar.

"I've noticed," Clay remarked dryly. "I figured that people would be surprised at first that we broke it off with Jesse. We haven't been back to town since seeing her touching moment on the sidewalk with her ex. But I thought once they saw her with him, they would realize that *she* had been the one who wanted out of the relationship."

"Jesus, Clay. What could we have done? Beg her not to go back to her ex husband? Do what we talked about and drag her kicking and screaming back to the ranch?"

"I don't know." Clay regarded his friends at the bar. "Disappointed," he murmured.

"What?"

"They're acting like we disappointed them somehow."

"How? What the fuck did we do?"

"I have no idea. But we're going to find out."

Rio looked up as Jake and Blade entered the bar, speaking lowly, their expressions grim. John and Michael moved to the end of the bar at their approach and handed each a beer. All of a sudden a heated discussion took place although they kept their voices low.

A few of the men at the bar, men he and his brother considered friends moved closer and listened attentively, nodding in response to whatever Jake said to them. He could see the concern and anger on their faces which confused him even more.

"I wonder what that's all about," Rio remarked, starting to get a bad feeling.

When the conversation at the bar ended, several eyes turned briefly in their direction before shifting away.

"That does it. I've had enough of this."

He waited impatiently as Jake and Blade made their way to their table. Neither man looked happy.

"What the fuck is going on?" Clay leaned forward, and Rio wasn't surprised by the fire in his eyes. "What was that discussion at the bar about? Why is everyone looking at Rio and me like we did something wrong?"

Rio eyed both men. "Why is the place so quiet? I've never been in here that the music wasn't playing with everyone talking or arguing about something?"

Jake sighed. "We haven't seen either one of you for a week. Every time I've gone up to the ranch you haven't been around. Your phones are off."

"We didn't want to talk to anybody," Rio grumbled.

"Well, whatever happened between you two and Jesse happened. But I promised not to talk to you about it, even though I think you're both a couple of idiots."

Rio shook his head in confusion. "You're pissed at us because Jesse wanted to go back to her husband?"

"What?" Jake and Blade both barked.

Clay and Rio glanced at each other.

"She invited him here. We heard her." Rio leaned forward. "We *saw* her with him."

Jake and Blade looked stunned which confused Rio even more.

"Listen," Blade began. When Jake started to speak Blade simply held up a hand. "I didn't promise Jesse that I wouldn't talk to Clay and Rio about her." His voice dipped. "And Kelly's in danger too."

"Danger?" Rio thundered. "Kelly?" Rio looked at his brother. "Isn't that Jesse's partner?"

At Clay's nod, Rio turned back to Blade. "Why are Jesse and Kelly in danger? What is going on, damn it?"

"Jesse never had any intention of going back to her ex-husband, you asshole." Blade directed his icy anger at his friends. "He's been bothering her for money, although she's trying to hide it. Kelly overheard a conversation they had. She thinks that Brian threatened Jesse."

Blade rubbed a hand over his face. "We can't find the bastard. But, we think he's on his way here."

Rio felt all the blood leave his face. "Why didn't you tell us? Are they alone?"

"We take turns going over there. Jesse figured out once that we'd been watching her and she threatened to move away. She doesn't want to *burden* any of us with her problems." Jake looked disgusted. "We can't very well protect her if she left and the two men that could have been with her kicked her out!"

Rio wanted to hit something and by the look on his brother's face, he felt the same way.

"Let's go get our woman," he told his brother. He stood and paused when Jake's cell phone rang. Jake jumped and answered on the first ring, his whole body tense.

"Kelly? What? Calm down! I can't understand you. *What!* I'm on my way!"

Clay and Rio watched Jake sprint for the door, Blade on his heels. Rio ran after them, Clay at his side. He noted that the men from the bar followed right behind them.

"What did Kelly say?" Blade demanded, not even winded.

"She said he's killing her. Brian's here and he's killing Jesse."

"Fuck!" Rio had never felt such fear in his life. *Someone was hurting his woman.* Rio tore down the street, adrenaline and fear making his legs pump like never before. He sensed his brother at his heels but he concentrated on nothing more than getting to Jesse.

When the building that Jesse had moved into came into view Rio heard the screams.

He hit the door without slowing, sending it flying as it literally flew off its hinges.

What he saw filled him rage.

A man backhanded a pretty young woman as she tried to pull him off Jesse. She went sprawling and the man reared back to punch an already bloody and barely conscious Jesse in the face.

Rio tackled the man just before his punch landed.

Rage like he had never felt before reddened his vision and he used his fists like a wild man. That someone would *dare* to lay a hand in *his* woman infuriated him.

That someone would hurt her agonized him.

He never felt the punches he landed. He only knew that he couldn't stop.

It took both Jake and Blade to pull him off the man who fell bloody and unconscious. The rage still burned inside him and he knew that he felt far from in control.

Then he heard Clay's voice.

"Rio, Jesse needs us."

The red haze disappeared.

He moved to kneel beside the woman he loved more than his own life.

And nearly wept.

She lay unconscious, her face battered and bloody, her right arm obviously broken.

"Oh, baby."

He leaned over her, unconsciously shielding her with his body as he touched her tenderly.

"An ambulance is on the way." Jake knelt next to Clay and Rio as they tried to rouse her, careful not to move her. "So is Ace." Rio knew Ace Tyler, the town sheriff, would be livid.

"I'm sorry I didn't get here sooner, honey," Jake murmured to an unconscious Jesse as he ran his hands over her looking for injuries.

Rio watched as Clay moved his hands over Jesse's legs, checking for breaks and couldn't help noticing that she had on another pair of those baggy pants she'd worn when they first met her. Why didn't she wear the things he and Clay had bought her?

"Why don't you check on Kelly and leave Jesse to us?" Clay gestured toward the other woman.

Jake shook his head. "Blade is looking after Kelly." He glanced over to see Blade helping Kelly to her feet, apparently against his better judgment. He looked ready to catch her if she fell but she insisted that she wanted to see Jesse.

Jake looked at his friends. "If Jesse wakes to find you here, she's going to be upset enough. I don't want her to wake to find you both with your hands all over her. Trust me when I tell you it would be too much for her right now."

"Jesus, Jake," Rio muttered. "We thought she wanted out." He couldn't stop touching his woman, careful of her injuries. Her poor face had already started to swell, her lip split.

Rio rose and went to the kitchen where he quickly dampened a towel and put ice in another. Her hurried back to tend his battered woman, anguish and fear tying his stomach in knots.

Kneeling next to Jesse, he placed the ice on her swollen eye, and using the dampened cloth, began to gently wipe the blood from her face so that they could better assess her injuries.

"What the fuck is going on, Jake?" Clay asked, clearly baffled. "Who is that guy? That's not the guy we saw her with."

Jake glanced up. "It's Brian, Jesse's ex. He's the one who's been threatening her, although she tried to hide it."

"Jesse!" Nat came rushing through the splintered doorway, the blood draining from her face when she saw her sister.

"Oh, my God! What happened?" She glanced over and saw the man on the floor. "That's Brian! He hurt her?"

"Everything will be fine now, Nat." Jake stood and put a comforting arm around his wife. "We're taking care of her." He hugged her to his chest, dropping a kiss on her head.

"I'm alright. I need to see Jesse."

Rio heard the other woman, Kelly, he remembered, and glanced over his shoulder. Blade frowned and held onto her as she rushed over. She shoved and would have knocked Clay over if he had been a smaller man.

"Oh, Jesse. Look what he did to you."

Then she did something that forever endeared her to him. She stomped over and kicked the now conscious Brian.

Ace walked in just in time to see it and although his eyes remained grim, his lips twitched.

"I take it this is the man who attacked Jesse," he asked dryly. He hauled Brian up with one hand and handed him off to his deputies who had walked in behind him.

"Get him to the ambulance and read him his rights. Stay with him. I'll be there as soon as I can."

When the deputies left with their charge, Ace turned to Jake. "There's an ambulance outside waiting for Jesse and Kelly."

"Tell the paramedics to hurry," Rio said before Jake could reply. "We've got to get them treated and make sure there are no internal injuries."

"I'm taking Kelly out now." Blade simply lifted the younger woman in his arms, overcoming her struggles with a "Stop it. I don't know where else you're hurt."

A gurney was wheeled inside, and before the paramedics could stop him, Rio lifted Jesse's slight weight in his arms, carefully cradling her and moved to the gurney.

He saw Clay hover anxiously, standing between Jesse and the paramedics as he warned him not to jostle her.

Everyone moved aside as the paramedics started to wheel her out. Just short of the doorway Jesse woke and gasped, grabbing her side.

Rio, the closest, stopped the gurney and leaned protectively over her.

"Everything's okay, darlin'. Clay and I are here. We're going to take good care of you."

Rio's beloved voice felt like warm honey dripping over her. She sighed and tried to open her eyes but couldn't seem to pry them open more than slits. Her side felt like she had been stabbed and her face throbbed. When she saw Rio she automatically started to reach for him and groaned as fire raced up her arm.

And she remembered.

She cradled her arm against her sore ribs and sobbed. "No! I didn't call you."

Clay leaned over her other side. Both he and Rio looked worried.

"Easy, baby," Clay whispered, touching her hair.

"Where's Kelly? Kelly!"

"Kelly's fine, honey. She's in the ambulance waiting for you. She's just going to get checked out. You're the one who's hurt."

"Jake," Jesse whimpered.

"I'm here, honey."

"Kelly. Hospital." She looked at Clay and Rio. "Go away."

* * * *

Clay turned from his position at the window as Kelly and Blade came out of the treatment room. He looked at his watch yet again and realized she'd been back there for over an hour. Blade walked beside her, his arm around her waist as he led her to a chair.

The men from the bar had finally gone after getting promises to call them when they knew something.

He and Rio waited, along with Nat and Jake. Ace drifted in and out talking on his radio while Blade traipsed back and forth from the room where they'd treated and released Kelly.

He started pacing again, anxious for word on Jesse and still more than a little confused.

Who had Jesse been talking to that day on the street? Why had Brian attacked her if they'd gotten back together?

He'd have to ask Kelly. He looked over at the young woman and almost smiled when he saw her glaring at Blade. Again.

Kelly had wanted to stay with Jesse and her objection to being treated ignored as Blade picked her up in his arms and carried her to the treatment room.

No one knew what had gone on between them but had an idea when Kelly glared at Blade whenever she caught his eyes on her.

Blade simply lifted a brow which had Kelly turning bright red and glancing away.

Clay finally stopped his pacing and faced everyone. He needed some answers.

"I don't understand any of this. Why would you think that we'd just kick Jesse out? We heard her phone conversation when she convinced her ex-husband to come and move in with her and told him that since Rio and I were so crazy about her, we'd go after anyone she sicced us on, even someone who came after him."

He sighed deeply. "We're in love with her and she betrayed us."

Rio slumped into a chair. "We came to town a few days after she left. We saw her on the sidewalk, outside the building she and Kelly are renting. We saw her talking with a man and it looked like they knew each other well. We saw a moving truck. He touched her hair."

"That was Cullen," Kelly said softly.

"Who is Cullen?" Clay asked carefully.

"My brother, who also happens to be like a brother to Jesse. He stayed with me while Jesse came out here. He helped us move."

"Helped *you* move? What happened to Brian? I thought *he* moved here."

"Of course not. Why would she want him to move here? She can't stand him."

"We *heard* her," Rio insisted. "She called him honey and said that she had found a place for them. We heard her begging him to move here."

"She had that conversation with me." Kelly jumped up only to have Blade settle her back into her chair.

"Don't jump like that. You're hurt," he told her.

"You?" Clay couldn't believe this! What else had they gotten wrong?

When Kelly motioned him over, Clay moved to sit next to her while Rio knelt at her feet.

Touching both of them on the arm, Kelly began. "This is something that I'd have preferred to keep quiet but to understand what's happened, you have to know."

Kelly's voice sounded raw and full of pain. "Jesse and I met because my ex boyfriend, Simon, is Brian's friend and sometimes partner. Brian and Simon are lazy and mean but could be completely charming when they chose to. As con men, their livelihood depended on it."

She sucked in a breath. "The difference between them was that until today, Brian never hit Jesse. Simon liked to use me for a punching bag."

Clay heard Blade's growl from the other side of Kelly but she ignored him.

"Jesse happened to come over once when Simon hit me."

She smiled as she remembered. "Jesse came in like an avenging angel. She jumped on Simon and beat the crap out of him. Boy, he looked stunned. She threw him out of the apartment we shared, tossed his stuff out the window and told him never to come back."

Tears filled her eyes. "She took me to the hospital, took me home with her, took care of me. Brian was away as usual. When he came back and found me staying in their house, he demanded that she take me back to my apartment and to stay out of it."

"She told him no and turned away. When he grabbed her arm and raised his fist, I thought, 'Oh God, he's going to hit her because of me.' Jesse never flinched. She's the type that didn't show her feelings. I thought she looked so cold when I first met her, but she's not at all. She uses it to hide. Only Alex and I got to see the real Jesse."

"Did he hit her?" Clay forced out.

Kelly shook her head. "No. Jesse just turned to him and cool as a cucumber told him to let go of her arm. Then Alex walked into the room. To this day I don't know if Jesse's cold look stopped him or if he stopped because his son walked into the room."

Kelly stood, shaking off Blade's restraining hand. "That was the end of their marriage."

Nat moved to wrap an arm around Kelly. "You know that you didn't cause it. Jesse and Brian had problems from the beginning. Since Brian stayed away so much, she hung in there, but only until Alex went away to college. And Brian knew it."

"That's what Jesse said, but I'd wondered." Kelly turned back to him and Rio. "She sounded so happy when she called. She said she loved it here and wanted to move our business and me here. She desperately wanted to stay. She talked about both of you and how much she wanted to be with you."

She grimaced. "I probably shouldn't be telling you this but she told me how much she loved you both, but didn't want you to feel pressured when you learned that she had moved here. She didn't want anything that you didn't want to give. She didn't think that you loved her."

Clay groaned and rubbed a hand over his face tiredly.

"But she wouldn't just leave me." Kelly told them. "I have to admit, I'm relieved. Not only because Simon is afraid of her but because Jesse and I have become very close. I love her. I was excited about coming here, but at the same time, it scared me."

"What scared you, sweetheart?" Blade asked tenderly.

Clay saw that Kelly's eyes looked as big as saucers as she looked at Blade.

"What if Simon follows me here? What if he goes after Jesse because she humiliated him? What if we didn't know anybody here who would help us? I didn't want to bring trouble with me. Jesse and I, well we just wanted a fresh start." Her voice broke.

Clay glanced over to find his brother watching him. He looked as miserable as Clay felt.

"She told you that if Simon showed up, Clay and I would take care of him, didn't she?" Rio asked, sighing.

Kelly nodded through her tears.

Clay leaned forward and rubbed his eyes. God, how could they have been so wrong?

"If Simon shows his face in Desire, I will take great pleasure in bashing it in for him," Clay told Kelly firmly.

"You'd have to get in line," Blade added and Clay couldn't help but notice Blade's clenched jaw and the way the hand resting on his thigh had tightened into a fist.

Clay stood and walked to the window, looking out but not seeing anything except Jesse's battered face.

Rio groaned. "Why didn't she tell us all of this?"

"Jesse didn't want anyone to know her plans until she talked to Kelly," Nat told him softly. "She wanted to make sure Kelly wanted to move out here. When Kelly said yes, she didn't know how to tell you without sounding like she expected something from you. She firmly believed that you didn't want a real relationship with her, that you only wanted sex."

"*Fuck*," Clay grimaced. "We sure fucked up, didn't we, Rio?"

"What do you mean?" Nat looked from one to the other.

"That's what we told her," Rio kicked a chair and sent it flying into the wall. He ran his hands over his face. "We didn't want her to see how much she hurt us. When we overheard her conversation, we told her that it *was* only sex and that she should leave."

"Oh, no!" Nat and Kelly exclaimed together.

"That's not all," Clay added grimly. "When we thought she wanted us to beat up the guy threatening Brian, we told her not to bother calling us when trouble followed her."

Jake stepped up to Clay and put a hand on his shoulder in sympathy.

"What a fucking mess."

"Yeah," Clay sighed and turned from the window. "Rio and I fucked up huge. We've got to make it up to her, make her forgive us."

"It's not going to be easy," Rio said as he paced. "But at least we know that she wanted to stay with us and had no interest in going back to Brian."

"Yeah, there's that."

"There's something you're forgetting, your biggest hurdle." Blade stood, his eyes never leaving Kelly's.

Clay saw Jake nod.

"What?" Rio asked.

Blade glanced at him, then back at Kelly. "You showed Jesse that you didn't trust her. Now she doesn't trust you. Without trust, you have nothing."

Rio slumped in his chair and looked at his brother, his eyes full of anguish.

"What have we done?"

Chapter 11

Jesse groaned. She hurt everywhere. Blinking her eyes open she saw both Clay and Rio leaning over her. She was lying in a hospital bed. It all came back in a rush.

"Are you in pain, baby?"

Jesse saw the concern and tenderness in Clay's eyes and fought not to respond to it. She remembered them being at the store after Brian attacked her.

What happened to Brian? Where's Kelly?

"Kelly?" Jesse tried to sit up, gasping when a knife sharp pain in her side stopped her.

"Easy, Jesse." Rio's voice sounded sandpaper rough, but his hands felt gentle as he and Clay settled her back to the bed.

"Kelly's here, baby. She's okay." Clay rubbed her shoulder soothingly.

"Jesse!"

Jesse watched Kelly rush over and winced when she saw the swelling and black eye on the right side of Kelly's face.

"Oh, Kelly. He hit you."

"I'm okay, Jesse. You're the one he hurt."

"I'm sorry." She swallowed, tears pricking her eyes. "What happened to Brian?"

"He's in jail," Rio snarled. "I should have killed him."

Nat shoved Clay aside to move closer, Jake at her side.

"Everything's okay, honey. How do you feel?"

"I'm fine." Jesse couldn't believe how weak her voice sounded.

Jake leaned forward. "You're not fine. You've got a broken arm, cracked ribs, a concussion and a face that somebody used as a punching bag."

His face looked murderous, but he stroked her hand tenderly below the cast on her arm.

"The sheriff's outside. You need to tell him what happened. Can you do that now?"

She tried to nod and pain shot through her skull. Keeping her head still, she waited for it to go away. "Yes, I'll talk to him."

"Good." Jake drew a deep breath. "I'm so sorry, honey. I'm sorry that I didn't protect you."

"It's not your fault. I told you I could take care of myself. I guess I didn't do such a good job, huh?"

Jesse looked away from the concern she saw on their faces. "I shouldn't have come here, shouldn't have had Kelly move here." She tried to clear the hoarseness from her throat. "I brought trouble here and made people unhappy. I never meant to push myself or my problems on all of you. I just liked it here so much that I thought it would be a good place to start over."

She looked over at Kelly. "I'm sorry that I made you come here. When I'm healed, we'll leave and find somewhere else to start over."

Jesse jumped when Clay, Rio, Blade and Nat all yelled. "No-O!"

Clay looked at the others and moved forward. "Rio and I are the ones who are sorry that we made such a big mistake in letting you go. We thought it was what you wanted. We're going to do everything we can to make it up to you. If we had been around, you wouldn't have gotten hurt."

Fire flashed in his eyes along with something that she couldn't quite believe as he loomed closer.

"You're stuck with us now and anyone who tries to hurt you is going to have to go through us to do it. You are *not* leaving. Make no mistake, Jesse. Rio and I will do everything in our power to stop you if you try."

"I don't understand." Jesse frowned. "Why did you think I wanted to leave you?"

Jake stepped forward. "The sheriff is waiting. Tell him what happened. You can talk to Clay and Rio later."

Ace Tyler loomed every bit as large as Clay, though about ten years younger. His rugged features could never be called handsome and there was something in his eyes that made a person feel as though he could see right through them.

Jesse could imagine that many criminals confessed their crimes while being impaled with the sheriff's sharp stare.

His eyes kindled with anger as he caught sight of her injuries but gentled as he seated himself next to her and met her gaze.

"Can you tell me what happened, Jesse?"

Jesse sighed and stared at the ceiling as a single tear trickled down her face.

"He's never hit me before. He just went crazy."

"Why did he come here, Jesse? I understand he's been calling you. Did he threaten you?"

Jesse glanced at Kelly and Nat.

"Tell him, Jesse." Nat fisted her hands on her hips. "Kelly and I knew about the calls even though you tried to hide it."

Jesse watched Nat pace back and forth, shooting daggers at her while she told the sheriff her story. She winced when her sister started rearranging the flowers they'd brought, slamming the baskets down on the windowsill. With the rough way Nat handled the poor flowers, she knew she'd be lucky to have a single bloom left.

"But lately he's been calling you?" the sheriff asked.

"Until recently, I hadn't heard from him in a while. He used to come around every now and then wanting me to give him money. I send most of it to Alex for school. I tell him that and he goes away."

"But this time was different?" Ace asked gently.

Another tear trickled down Jesse's face and she hurriedly wiped it away. She told the sheriff about Brian's visit to Alex. "I didn't want him anywhere around Alex, especially with someone after him. I had to tell him where I am."

Clay turned from the window and Jesse saw such anger on his face she flinched. His eyes gentled on hers when he saw it and Rio continued to rub her hand.

The sheriff looked up from his notepad.

"Kelly, did you see him when he came looking for Jesse?"

"No," Kelly shook her head. "Cullen wouldn't let him near me."

"Thank God," Jesse heard Blade murmur from across the room.

"Alex! I've got to call Alex." Jesse tried to sit up and hissed when the pain in her side froze her in place.

Clay rushed across the room to her. "Baby, please lay back down. Kelly already talked to Alex. She told him that you had a little accident, but that you're fine and would call him in a day or two."

Clay gently but firmly settled her, pulling the light blanket back over her. She swallowed a sob. How she'd missed his touch.

"How long ago did he find out where you are?" Ace asked softly.

Jesse could see his anger at what had happened and that he tried not to upset her any more.

"About a week ago."

"Has he contacted you since then?"

Jesse closed her eyes and leaned back on the pillows. "Every day. He calls and demands money. He sounded more and more desperate every time he called."

"And you didn't think you should tell me about it?" Jake demanded angrily.

Jesse met his gaze unflinchingly. "I didn't want you to worry."

"My hand is just itching to paddle your ass," he said through clenched teeth, making Jesse wince.

"No longer your responsibility." Clay tossed his statement over his shoulder from where he stood next to her bed with his hands crossed over his chest. "From now on, we'll deal with her."

Jesse frowned at Clay, who met her look squarely.

"Tell me what happened tonight."

She turned her head at the sheriff's question. She closed her eyes as she replayed it in her head.

She opened her eyes and looked at him. "Kelly and I had just finished one of the displays. I heard a knock at the door. I thought it was Nat. I got distracted and opened the door without thinking. He barged in and slammed me against the counter." Jesse looked down at the cast on her arm and shivered. "My arm broke. I couldn't fight him."

She felt Clay's lips on her hair. "It's okay, baby. You're safe now."

"I yelled at Kelly to run, to get help."

Kelly stepped forward. "I grabbed Jesse's cell phone and ran in the back to call Jake. He made sure that his number had been programmed in her phone. And Jake told me to call if we ever needed him. After I called Jake, I ran back to try to help Jesse. I ran in just in time to see Brian knock her down and kick her in the side." Kelly shuddered. "He picked her up and when I tried to pull him off of her he slapped me back and all hell broke loose."

The sheriff had a few more questions and when everyone had finished telling their part in the story, he stood.

"I'm not going to have any problem keeping him locked up." He eyed Jesse. "You just worry about getting well."

When Jesse closed her eyes, Clay saw Ace's gaze touch each of the men and gesture toward the door.

The men filed out behind the sheriff. Clay leaned close to Jesse. "I'm just going to have a word with Ace. I'll be right back."

Out in the hallway Ace stood with his hands on his hips. His eyes no longer looked gentle as they had while he questioned Jesse. Now they glittered diamond hard.

"We have a big problem."

"Yeah," Clay saw Rio nod and rub the back of his neck, his voice rough. "We still have whoever Brian conned looking for his money. If he trailed Brian here, Jesse and Kelly are still in danger."

Clay nodded. "I'm calling Lucas. I'm going to have him and his men put in a top of the line security system for the girls. Rio and I are going to be watching them like hawks."

"Good idea." Ace nodded. "But we all need to stay sharp. I'm going to see if I can find out who this guy is. We'll be better prepared if we know what he looks like and can keeps tabs on him."

Jake leaned back against the wall and scrubbed a hand tiredly over his face. "The girls have worked their asses off all week to get the store ready to open. Now it's in shambles."

"We'll clean it up. I want to get it done before Jesse sees it." Clay looked toward the door of Jesse's room. "I don't want to leave her alone though."

Blade spoke for the first time. "Kelly is adamant about staying here with Jesse tonight. I'll stay and watch over them. When Jesse's released tomorrow, I'll bring them both back."

Clay watched Blade shift restlessly, running a hand repeatedly through his hair and over his face. His usually calm and cool friend looked anything but. He knew Blade hated abuse of a woman in any form but it appeared Kelly's involvement had him especially upset.

He understood how he felt.

"Christ, I hate this," Clay muttered. "I don't want to leave her."

A nurse came down the hall carrying a tray full of medications and entered Jesse's room.

"Whatever they give her will probably knock her out for the night anyway." Jake slapped a hand on Rio's shoulder. "Come on, let's say goodnight before they knock her out. I'll take Nat home and help you clean up."

Clay and Rio worked through the night. They'd sent Jake home several hours earlier to be with Nat. At the hospital she'd argued to no avail when the nurses had asked her to leave. They didn't want more than one person with Jesse and she knew that Kelly needed to be there.

When they'd told Blade to leave, one angry glare had them backing off.

Clay had called Lucas in to set up the security system. When Lucas heard what had happened, he'd been outraged. Within the hour he had arrived with his two partners, Devlin and Caleb, and they installed an elaborate system, working well into the night.

Clay and Rio spent the time cleaning up the mess in the store and helping with the alarm system. When the hardware store opened early the next morning, they bought a new front door which then had to be added to the security system. They also bought the supplies they needed to rebuild shelves that had been damaged.

They had a lot of help as the men around town heard what happened. Many stopped by to help and with so many hands, the work went quickly.

When Gracie showed up with her three adoring husbands with coffee and breakfast sandwiches for everyone, Clay and Rio looked at them in astonishment.

"Gracie, you didn't have to do this," Clay told her tenderly.

"That's what friends are for." Gracie smiled at him. "We're all in it together here. Didn't you show up when the water pipe burst in the diner? Didn't you come and help us clean that mess up?" She glanced at Rio. "Now I suppose you're going to tell me that the two of you know nothing about all that new equipment that showed up. Everybody in this room chipped in for that and not one of you will admit to it or take a cent for it."

She looked back at Clay. "So if I want to bring some coffee and sandwiches to some hungry men, I don't want to hear another word about it."

Garrett, one of Gracie's husbands stepped forward. "We all know what you people did for us and we appreciate it more than you know. We would have been out of business without that equipment."

Drew, another of her husbands, nodded. "We know there are a lot of people in this town with money to burn, but not one of you is ever snobby with it. You're always there to help." He looked at Clay. "This is such a little thing to do and we feel so bad about what happened to the women."

Finn, Gracie's third husband, started handing out coffee. "We've gotten soft. We need to keep a closer watch on our women." He glanced at his wife. "Maybe we should put leashes on them."

Of course Gracie told him what he could do with his leash, effectively lightening the tension and everyone laughed as they helped themselves to breakfast.

"You're in the doghouse now," Clay heard Rio mutter to Finn under his breath.

"Yeah," Finn agreed, not looking too worried. "But I know our woman well and I know how to get out of the doghouse." He slapped Clay on the back. "Now that you and Rio have found your woman, you'll see what I mean. Once she gets over being mad, I mean it was just a little misunderstanding." He looked over his shoulder at his wife and lowered his voice, "You'll find out just how much fun it is to piss your woman off and get her to forgive you."

Jake spoke from behind them. "Finn, don't you think Clay and Rio have enough to do to get themselves out of the hot water they're already in without giving them advice on making more trouble?"

Finn laughed. "A woman with a temper makes life worth living. Making her mad adds spice to life."

Rio leaned forward and whispered. "Gracie heard that."

Finn blanched. "Fuck."

Clay, Rio and Jake roared with laughter as Finn looked over his shoulder to his frowning wife.

"Let's see how spicy your life is when you're sleeping on the sofa," Gracie retorted.

Garrett came forward. "You've done it again, Finn. I swear Drew and I spend half our lives trying to get you out of trouble. You go on over and try to get out of it yourself this time."

Garrett shook his head. "It's going to be a long day at the diner with those two." His eyes shifted between Clay and Rio. "I thought the two of you had dumped that sweet girl and I wanted to pound on the both of you. When Jake explained what had happened, well, that must have hurt like hell to think that she wanted someone else."

He sighed. "I don't know what I would have done if that would have happened to us. You boys are going to have to work on getting her trust back and let me tell you, that's not going to be easy."

He looked at his wife of almost thirty years and grimaced. "Do yourself a favor and let her know just what she means to you. Don't try to hide what you feel for her. If you haven't told her that you're crazy in love with her yet, do it."

Clay nodded. "Thanks. For everything."

Clay's cell rang as he watched Garrett move away.

"We'll be leaving in just a few minutes." Blade sounded tired.

"Bring them to the ranch. We're just about finished here. Either Rio or I will come back and finish up, but I want Jesse to go straight to bed when she gets there."

The men in the room listened attentively to his conversation and nodded their agreement.

"Uh, I don't think Jesse's going to like that." Blade chuckled. "Got a nice temper going on here."

Clay grinned. "I've never seen you intimidated by a woman's temper before." He heard chuckles from the others.

"Oh, it's not me she's pissed at."

"Good. Better to get it all out from the start. How is she?"

"Sore and tired and trying very hard not to show it," Blade replied softly. "And she wants to go back to the apartment."

Clay sobered. "Do you know she's been sleeping on a fucking cot? How the hell is she supposed to get better sleeping on a cot?

She's bruised all over! Cracked ribs, a broken arm. There's no way we're going to let her stay in that apartment. She can stay with us. So can Kelly. I don't want her here alone."

"Kelly wants to go back to the apartment." Blade sighed. "She wants to get everything ready before Jesse has a chance to see how much stuff got broken. Is the alarm system in?"

"Yeah, and it's a beaut," Clay replied with a glance at Lucas. "A mouse couldn't get in without setting it off."

"Good. Here they come. See you in a few."

Everyone left the store and Clay and Rio had just enough time to get back to the ranch and shower before Blade pulled in.

Kelly sat up front with Blade, a stony look on her face and Jesse lay curled up on the back seat.

Jesse stirred when the big SUV stopped and blinked when she saw Rio open the door and reach for her. Still groggy, she felt herself being gently lifted and pulled from the truck.

"We're at your ranch. *Stop.* " She struggled then froze as the knife pain went through her side.

"There's no use fighting us, darlin'. You're here and you're staying here." Rio entered the house and moved quickly to the bedroom.

"I don't want to be here." Her eyes met Blade's, but he only shook his head.

"Your men will look after you. You're safe here to heal."

"They're not my men. I want to go to the apartment with Kelly."

"To sleep on a fucking cot?" Rio roared.

Clay glared at his brother. "Kelly can stay here, too," he said as he knelt and removed her shoes.

"No, I want to go to the apartment." Kelly brushed the men aside and took Jesse's uninjured hand in hers. "I have the car you bought. I'll come to visit you. Blade says that Clay and Rio had a security system set up for the whole building. Clay and Rio and a bunch of other people spent all night there cleaning the place up."

The two men met Jesse's gaze calmly.

"Why would you do that?"

Clay folded his arms across his chest. "You're ours and we protect what belongs to us. You can fight about it as much as you want but there it is."

"I want to finish settling in and work on getting more stuff made before we open," Kelly continued, jerking Jesse's attention back to her.

"You've taken care of me for so long, Jesse. Please let me finish getting the store ready while you heal. Please let me do this for you."

Jesse knew Kelly needed to stand on her own two feet and any argument she made would just sound selfish but she felt uneasy about Kelly being there alone.

"I should still be there so you're not alone."

Kelly raised a brow questioningly. "How quickly do you think you're going to heal trying to sleep on that cot? I know you won't take my bed. Plus, you know how distracted I get when I'm in the workroom. What if you needed me and I didn't hear you? What if I didn't pay attention to the time and you went too long without your pain medicine? I would never forgive myself if you spent hours in pain because I got distracted."

She shook her head. "I'd never get anything done if I worried about you. If you stay here, Clay and Rio would be able to take care of you. They could carry you so you didn't hurt yourself and they would make sure that you're fed and comfortable. You can bet that they'll make sure you have your pain medicine on time."

Jesse saw Clay frown. "I think you should still come here to sleep. If you want to spend your days at the store, fine, but I don't like the thought of you there by yourself at night."

"I'll be looking after her." Blade met Kelly's eyes mockingly.

"I don't need you to look after me."

Rio shook his head. "Jesse's ours and you're Jesse's so you're ours also. Either you listen to Blade and let him look after you or you'll be coming back here at dark every night even if one of us has to drag you kicking and screaming. You know very well that we'll do it."

"Well, what's it going to be, Kelly?" Blade asked smugly.

"Kelly," Jesse could barely keep her eyes open. "I won't be able to rest comfortably if I'm worried about you. You wouldn't want me to lose sleep and not heal as fast because I'm scared that something could happen to you, would you?"

When Kelly sighed, Jesse knew she'd won. "Fine. Blade can look after me."

"You'll listen to him. Won't you Kell?"

"Yes, Jesse."

"Thanks, honey. As soon as I feel better, a couple of days at the most, I'll be back," Jesse felt sleep began to overtake her.

"Of course you will," She heard Kelly say and went out.

Clay left Kelly to unpack Jesse's things they'd brought from the apartment and walked outside to join Rio and Blade.

He looked at Blade. "Lucas is waiting to hear from you. Call him and he'll meet you to explain the system to you and Kelly." Clay handed him a folded piece of paper. "Here's the code to get in."

He reached into his shirt pocket and pulled out a thin black square, rubbing his thumb over the smooth surface as he eyed Blade.

"Are you as crazy about Kelly as you look?"

"Christ, am I that transparent?" Blade muttered in disgust.

"Only to someone who feels the same way about a woman."

"Yeah," Blade nodded. He scraped a hand through his long hair. "Here I am, a Dom for Christ's sake and what kind of woman do I fall for? One that's been physically and emotionally abused. One who's afraid of men. She won't even let me touch her. Ain't that a kick in the ass?"

Clay put a hand on Blade's shoulder. For a man like Blade, who had always been too good looking for his own good and who had women constantly throwing themselves at him, begging him to be their Dom, to fall in love with a woman who's afraid of his touch was just pure irony.

"Well, you always liked a challenge. This one should keep you on your toes," Rio told Blade, chuckling.

"Don't laugh." Blade slapped Rio on the shoulder. "You have your own challenge ahead of you."

Clay saw Rio sober. "If that ain't the truth. Man, women never used to be such work."

Clay regarded his brother and good friend. "Yeah, but when they wrap themselves around your heart, they're worth it, whatever it takes."

When both Rio and Blade nodded Clay held out the black square to Blade.

"What's this?" Blade looked at the square and back to Clay.

"It's a remote that will alert you when the security's been breached in the women's building. Rio and I each have one and when I saw the way you looked at Kelly, I had Lucas program another one for you."

"Thanks." Blade regarded the square thoughtfully. "I'm going to check in with Ace after I drop Kelly off. I want to know where Simon is too."

Clay nodded grimly. "With Brian in jail, at least we don't have to worry about him. I also have Lucas on this so you might want to check with him, too."

"I'll stop by there, too. We keep each other posted, right?"

"Absolutely." Rio nodded.

"I don't want the women to know about this. I don't want them to worry," Clay added.

The others nodded but didn't get a chance to say anything because Kelly walked out the front door.

"I'm ready to go," she told Blade, not quite meeting his eyes. She turned toward Clay and Rio. Her eyes narrowed as she poked Clay in the chest. "You'd better take care of Jesse. And fix what you did to her."

"We will. I promise," Clay told her, kissing her forehead. "Don't worry about it. It's just a misunderstanding."

"You broke her heart," Kelly countered. "I've never heard her happy before. I never thought to see her like that."

A tear trickled from her eye and she hastily brushed it away and pointed angrily at both he and Rio.

"You get it back."

Chapter 12

Jesse couldn't remember ever being so comfortable in her life. Over her objections, Clay and Rio had stripped and bathed her, even washing and drying her hair, all the while carefully keeping her cast dry and cautious of her other injuries.

Their eyes hardened when they saw the bruises all over her body as they carefully tended to her.

She wore one of their huge soft cotton shirts, one that allowed her cast to slip through the sleeve. Propping her on a mountain of pillows, they'd fed her scrambled eggs and toast, even having the apple juice that she loved, before giving her the pain medication the hospital had sent home with her.

They settled her, making sure she was comfortable and they hovered over her, reaching for her each time she moved.

"Do you hurt anywhere, baby?" Clay settled a light blanket over her. "Are you cold?"

"I'm fine," Jesse slurred for about the hundredth time.

Rio leaned over to brush his finger lightly over her still swollen lips, his eyes full of regret.

"Do you understand why we let you go, Jesse? That it's what we thought you wanted?"

They had told her everything they'd heard and felt when they overheard her phone conversation with Kelly.

"I understand," Jesse told them tiredly. It got harder and harder to keep her eyes open.

"Then you know we love you?" Rio asked her.

Clay lifted her good hand. Turning it, he kissed her p holding hers. "We both love you very much, so much killed us to let you walk away. We're so sorry that we tl .... , .. . betrayed us."

"You didn't trust me. Can't love me." She struggled to stay awake. She had to make them understand but concentrating became difficult. "Can't love you anymore. You'll make me weak."

Clay looked at his brother in frustration. The pain medication had knocked her out with nothing settled between them. She wouldn't let them close to her again.

"What the hell did she mean by that," Rio asked angrily. "How the hell are we going to make her weak?"

"I have no idea, but while she's here with us she can't very well get up and leave. We'll have to use this time with her to try to fix what we fucked up before she has the chance to heal and walk away." Clay stood and tucked the blanket securely around her, the love he felt for her bringing a lump to his throat. "While she's asleep we'd better check in with Ace and Lucas, see if they have any news for us. I want to find Simon and the guy that Brian conned money from. Maybe Ace got it out of him."

"I hope so" he heard Rio say and turned to see his brother touch his lips to Jesse's forehead before turning to follow him. "We also need to check in with Blade and one of us has to drive over and see how Kelly's doing, see if anything needs to be done. It's the first thing that Jesse's going to be worried about when she wakes up."

"I'll go," Clay told him when they entered the kitchen. "I'll stop and see Ace and try to have a talk with his prisoner, see if we can find out anything. You call Lucas and see what he learned. I'll stop and see Kelly and make sure she's okay and see if she needs anything moved. If Blade's not over there, I'll stop and see him."

He looked toward the bedroom where Jesse lay sleeping. "You take care of her. She can have another pain pill in four hours if she wakes up. I should be back by then, but—"

"I think I can manage to take care of her," Rio frowned as he opened the refrigerator. "Buy some more apple juice while you're in town. Jesse sure does love that stuff and the doctor said that the pain medicine might make her feel thirsty."

"I'll buy friggin' truckloads of the stuff if it would keep her here," Clay told Rio somberly as he picked up his keys and headed out the door.

* * * *

The next several days went by quickly. Jesse slept quite a bit and she knew she owed her rapid healing to Clay and Rio. They watched her constantly and made sure she ate and took her medicine and generally took care of her.

Although they'd tried many times to get her to talk to them about their relationship, she adamantly refused to discuss it.

When they'd hovered over her like they would a child she'd become frustrated and snapped at them. They'd looked so hurt that she'd apologized and relented. It only reinforced her belief that if she let them have their way, she would become weak, totally dependant on them for everything.

She had made up her mind years ago that she would never put herself in that position again.

They took her to the local doctor for her follow up appointment, carrying her to the truck against her objections. Being with a large man, let alone two large men, meant that they tended to win most arguments simply by picking her up and putting her wherever they wanted her to be.

"Listen," she told them on the way to the doctor's office, "I am perfectly capable of walking. If you carry me into the doctor's office, you're going to embarrass me."

"Why?" Rio asked her frowning.

"Because," she sighed. "I'm not helpless."

"Nobody ever said that you're helpless, baby," Clay pointed out. "But, you are hurt. Why shouldn't we try to help you when we can?"

"But, I'm supposed to walk. I'll heal faster if I walk." She raised a brow. "You *do* want me to get better, don't you?"

"Of course we want you to get better," Clay snapped. "If the doctor says that you should be walking around, then you'll be walking around. Until then, we'll carry you wherever you need to go."

"No more carrying me to the bathroom." Jesse looked at both of them belligerently.

Rio cocked a brow. "Well, I guess that depends on what the doctor says, doesn't it?"

Jesse rolled her eyes, but had no choice as Rio carried her into the doctor's office. The doctor smiled when he saw them walk in with her, but apparently thought nothing of them carrying her.

Alone in the room, she got undressed and donned the gown the nurse had given her for her exam. When the doctor walked into the room she couldn't help but ask why he hadn't seemed surprised that she'd been carried in.

The kindly doctor chuckled. "I've been practicing medicine in this town for almost twenty years. You have no idea the lengths the men in this town will go to when one of their women is sick or hurt." He smiled and leaned toward her conspiratorially. "Watch this." He leaned back and spoke in his normal tone. "Well, young lady, what have you done to yourself?"

The door burst open and both Clay and Rio came into the room, looking anxious. The doctor met Jesse's frown with a wink.

"Is she okay, Doc?" Clay moved forward to stand next to Jesse's head.

"I haven't had a chance to look her over yet. Are you two staying?"

"Of course, we're staying. We would have been in here sooner, but the nurse waylaid us with paperwork." Rio sat in the lone chair in the room, moving it so he could see.

After the exam, in which the doctor did say that she should be walking around more and more, thank God, Clay and Rio stayed to help her get dressed. They had hounded the poor doctor through the entire thing, asking so many questions she thought she would die of embarrassment.

The doctor had regarded their overprotectiveness with a nonchalance that amazed her. If he saw nothing unusual about it, the men in this town must be more overprotective than she had given them credit for.

It angered her that a warm feeling took root in her heart at their protective attitude, even as she seethed that they thought her helpless and in need of that protecting.

What the hell had happened to her that she should get a warm fuzzy because they treated her like she needed to be coddled?

She'd proven over and over through the years that she could take care of herself, hadn't she? Why then, did she get an inner warmth when these two men, her lovers, took such good care of her?

She thought about it as they drove to the store. She'd convinced them that she needed to go and would get Kelly or Nat to come pick her up if they wouldn't take her.

After looking at each other in resignation, they'd relented.

When they pulled up in front of the store, Jesse got out and looked up at the new sign. They had named the store *Indulgences*. It would be opening the following week and Jesse wanted to get back to it. Neither Clay nor Rio allowed her to come here until the doctor okayed it.

Kelly smiled when she saw her and Jesse noticed her friend's amusement at Clay and Rio's hovering.

Jesse looked over her shoulder at her men. "We'll be in the back for a while. Why don't you guys go on home? Thanks for everything. I'll be all right now."

Rio frowned as Clay stepped forward. "If you think you're not coming home with us, you're sadly mistaken, honey. We'll be waiting right here. You shouldn't be out long today anyway. We'll bring you back tomorrow."

Jesse blew out a frustrated breath and spun to join Kelly in the back, wincing as her ribs protested.

"You're not as healed as you'd like to believe," she heard Clay from behind her.

"We'll be waiting. Don't take too long," Rio warned. "You're not strong enough yet to do too much."

When Jesse huffed and went into the back, the men roamed around the store looking at all the dainty little bottles. Clay couldn't claim to be entirely comfortable around all the little bottles but some he recognized from Jesse's things in their master bathroom.

He watched as Rio began picking up sample bottles from a display.

"Clay, look what I found." He grinned mischievously.

"What is it?" Clay walked over and took the bottle Rio handed him.

"It's peach scented and flavored massage oil."

"Really?" Clay inspected the small sample bottle, opening the top to smell the oil and smiled. The smell of peaches now always gave him a hard-on.

He looked over at his brother. "After what Jesse's been through, I'm sure a full body massage would make her feel better."

"Absolutely." Rio looked around until he found a supply of the scented oil on the shelves. "We'd better get a few extra. You never know when we might need them."

"True." Clay turned one of the bottles over to see the discreet price tag on the bottom. Counting out the money, he laid it beside the cash register while Rio put their purchase in one of the bright purple bags by the counter.

Jesse walked back into the front room and didn't trust the grins on Clay and Rio's faces. Her eyes narrowed. She knew those grins usually meant trouble. She frowned when she saw the bag in Rio's hand.

"What's that?"

"You made your first sale, darlin'" He pointed to the money by the register. "Your stuff is so good it sells itself."

"What happened? Did you run out of lilac scented hand cream?"

"No, darlin'. I'm crazy for the peach stuff." He wagged his brows suggestively.

"Idiot," she muttered and saw Clay grin.

"Ready to go?"

"I'm going to stay here."

"No, Jesse. You're not."

"Listen, both of you. This is where I live and I'm staying. I appreciate all you've done for me but it's time I came back here with Kelly."

"So you can sleep on a cot?" Clay thundered. "You live with us now."

"You told me that you let me go before because you thought that I wanted to go." Jesse waved her good arm at him angrily. "Now that I'm telling you that I want to go, you won't let me. What is it with you two?"

Clay started to step toward her but Rio put a hand out and moved to her instead.

"Honey, we thought you loved someone else. There's a big difference in letting someone go when you love them and want them to be happy and letting someone go because they're too headstrong to realize that they're fighting something that doesn't need to be fought."

She felt his hands smooth over her hair as his eyes held hers. "We love you, darlin' and we know that you love us." When she opened her mouth to speak, he put a finger to her lips, silencing her. "You're not ready to admit it yet but we know it just the same. You aren't ready to forgive us for the way we hurt you yet. We know that and we'll wait for as long as it takes for you to work it out in that hard head of yours." His finger traced her lips. "The one thing we will not do is let you go again. You live with us now and that's where you'll stay."

"You can't make me!"

"*Bet me.*" Clay pushed forward and didn't stop until he stood only inches away and lowered his face to hers.

"I'll carry you out of here without breaking a sweat." He put his finger to her lips as Rio had when she started to speak. "If you're going to argue about this whenever we bring you here, you won't be coming back."

"You can't keep me from my own store."

"You know better than that, Jesse. I can and will. Hell, I can have this store closed down if I want to."

He sighed. "Baby, I know that Rio and I fucked up. If we didn't love you so damned much that it terrified us that you wanted to leave, we wouldn't have acted the way we did."

Jesse's jaw dropped and she quickly snapped it shut.

"It's just sex," she stammered.

Clay stared at her for several long moments then nodded as if coming to a decision. "If that's all you'll give us for now, we'll take it."

Jesse gasped as Clay lifted her.

"But…" she began.

"You said it darlin'," Rio told her with a wink at Kelly, who stood in the doorway and grinning from ear to ear. "We'll take the sex for now but we won't stop until we have it all."

Seated between Clay and Rio on the way back to the ranch, Jesse couldn't help remembering the first night that they took her there.

She trembled, remembering how she'd felt and what they'd done to her that night. They'd done so much more since then. Just being around them made her weak with longing. Her nerves hummed just below the surface of her skin when they came near, caressed into heat at the sounds of their voices.

The scent of their skin made her nipples hard and her pussy clench before they ever touched her. It went way beyond wanting. They made her feel alive in a way she'd never felt before. It thrilled her and scared her to death.

As she lay in the cot all those nights, thinking of them, she came to a realization, something she couldn't talk about yet.

Loving them had opened her up to a hurt that she thought she'd never get over. She hadn't let herself open up to anyone except Alex and Nat, and to some extent Kelly, for so long that she'd almost forgotten the pain of doing so.

She'd sworn to herself that she'd never allow it to happen again and yet she had. She hadn't been able to keep up the barriers that Clay and Rio seemed determined to tear down. She feared that loving them would bring her more pain than she could ever imagine, but that they'd keep tearing down barriers until she had no choice but to give them everything.

The way they coddled her had her worried. How could she survive if they didn't let her take care of herself? Sure, it was nice to have a shoulder to lean on when you needed it but she didn't want to always be leaning on someone. Could she make them understand that she needed to be her own person, not just someone for them to put on a shelf wrapped in cotton and take down to play with whenever they got the urge?

She knew that they had to talk but she couldn't. Not yet.

Sex. That would be it. This time she promised herself that she wouldn't allow them to rip down those barriers she frantically patched. After all, how could she trust them not to turn her away again?

If they wanted sex, fine. Why the hell not? They were great in bed. God knew she responded to them like she had never responded to anyone else. She hadn't had orgasms for the last twenty years of marriage. She hid a grin. She didn't have that problem anymore.

She'd give them her body, but she wouldn't make the mistake of giving more than that.

Even before they'd tossed her out, there'd been no talk of something more permanent. Fine. If they wanted sex, that's all they'd get.

When they reached the ranch, no one spoke as they walked through the house. Jesse walked straight to the bedroom and started to undress.

Clay walked into the room with a stack of towels which he began to spread on the bed. Rio looked through the bag he'd brought from the store, pulling out one of the bottles and opening it.

Massage oil.

Jesse recognized the bottle. Standing naked, her body hummed with arousal. When they'd finished their tasks, both stared at her as they removed their boots and their shirts before reaching for her.

They helped her onto her stomach on the big bed. Now she knew why they'd put down the towels. Jeez, how much oil did they plan to use?

They settled her casted arm on a pillow and brushed her hair aside.

She trembled. Her nipples had already pebbled, her pussy wet as her body recognized her lovers and knew that indescribable pleasure would be coming soon.

She felt the first trickle of oil from the top of her spine all the way to her buttocks. Four strong hands massaged the oil into the tight back muscles, firmly coaxing the tension from them. Jesse could feel her sore muscles loosening and she groaned as they became lax.

The feeling of her skin being too tight, the prickles of sparks wherever they touched her made a stark contrast to the way her muscles became so loose they felt almost fluid.

More oil trickled from her thighs to her ankles. She felt Clay and Rio's callused hands as they rubbed the oil into her feet.

They relaxed and tantalized her at the same time. They aroused her bit by bit, the journey slow and steady but at the same time keeping her so loose she could do nothing but surrender to it.

She tried to press her legs together to relieve the overwhelming ache that had settled in her pussy, but they kept them apart, massaging her calves and holding them firmly in the position they wanted.

They made her sore body sing with pleasure as they worked out the aches and replaced them with tingles of destructive pleasure.

Her pussy wept, her moaning continuous by the time they reached her thighs. Strong hands soothed the oil into her. She groaned when they massaged her inner thighs. Her legs opened even wider.

When she felt the cheeks of her bottom being massaged and spread, she couldn't hold back a gasp. Oil trickled over her anus and she groaned as she felt it being gently massaged into her tight opening. She tensed when she experienced the always surprising, always forbidden feel of the plug being slowly pushed into her.

"Relax, baby. Remember how good it feels."

The massage continued on her bottom cheeks and thighs and Jesse couldn't keep from relaxing her muscles under those talented hands. Every time she relaxed a little more, they took advantage and pushed the plug further and further inside her tight anus.

She felt her body give as it entered her, the feeling of fullness making the muscles in her anus and pussy clench and her clit throb. When the widest part of the plug passed the tight ring of muscle, she squirmed, trying to rub her throbbing clit against the towels, but they held her thighs apart too far for her to get what she needed. She felt the plug narrow and the base firmly pushed against her as the plug entered her fully.

"That's my girl," Clay crooned, as they continued to massage her bottom and thighs.

"Please," Jesse whimpered. She felt completely relaxed and yet so tense at the same time made it difficult for her to breathe.

It felt like nothing that she had ever experienced, her body lost in a wave of pleasure that had her lax and quivering, so boneless that she didn't have the strength to move. Her anus and pussy burned, the juices from her pussy flowing as her anus clenched on the plug. Her nipples beaded and became so sensitive that the friction from the towel almost sent her into orgasm.

And her clit, oh, God, her clit throbbed with the need to be stroked. She knew that just one touch would send her into orbit.

"We're going to please you, darlin'." Tender hands turned her over, settling her right arm carefully back onto a pillow at her side.

Jesse closed her eyes against the sensation of the oil being poured over her breasts. With her good arm, she tried to reach for them, to rub her sensitive nipples missing the stimulation from the towel, but Clay caught her hand before she could reach them and kissed her fingers before lowering her arm back to the bed.

"No, baby. Just lie still. Let us do all the work. Let us make you feel good."

She pried her eyes when Rio began to massage the oil into her breasts, rubbing against the pebble hard nipples. She automatically arched into his caress, and watched his eyes flare.

She saw Clay move down the bed and between her thighs, shifting his broad shoulders to widen her further. His eyes locked with hers as he lowered his head.

"It's been far too long since I tasted my woman's pussy. I'm going to lap up all this sweet juice." He ran a finger along her slit and into her pussy opening.

"When he's finished," Rio growled, forcing her gaze to him, "it's my turn."

Jesse's eyes fluttered closed when she felt Clay's mouth on her. She would have thrashed, but Rio's hand held her still as she came almost immediately.

"Oh, God, what are you doing to me?" she wailed.

Rio bent down to lick a peach flavored nipple. "Loving you, darlin', just loving you."

Rio's attention stayed on her breasts. He rubbed and pinched and suckled, praising her response to his and Clay's ministrations, murmuring about how much he had grown to love peaches.

Clay's used his diabolical mouth on her relentlessly, seeming determined to make up for lost time. When his attention moved to her clit, Jesse sobbed brokenly as he forced another orgasm from her.

"No more, please. I can't take anymore."

Clay lifted his head. She watched as he licked his lips, still shiny with her juices.

"You are delicious, baby."

"My turn." Rio quickly moved down to the end of the bed and nudged Clay aside. "I hope you saved some for me."

"Make your own little brother."

Clay chuckled as he took his place at her breasts. "I've missed these breasts, too." He pinched a nipple and smiled when she gasped and arched into his hand. "And these sensitive little nipples."

"I can't come anymore." She tried to close her thighs, but with Rio's broad shoulders between them, she couldn't.

"*Bullshit,*" Rio growled. "You're *going* to come again, this time with my mouth on this sweet pussy."

"Let me have a taste of these peach flavored berries," Clay said to her softly as he bent to suck a nipple into his mouth.

With Rio's coaxing mouth on her slit, his tongue arrowing into her pussy and Clay's hands and mouth on her breasts, Jesse quivered as her arousal built once again. It burned hotter and hotter with each caress until she feared that the bed would go up in flames, burning them all with the fire they had unleashed in her.

Rio seemed to glory in every drop of juice that flowed from her, lapping as though starved for the taste of her.

The need these men seemed to have for her added yet another layer to an arousal so intense she didn't know if she could bear it. She thrashed as though trying to throw off the fury of her body's response to her lovers.

Digging her heels into Rio's shoulders, she bucked and came so hard that it actually scared her. Her vision dimmed and she screamed against the fierce orgasm that seemed to come from deep within her soul. Her body started to bow. Clay held her down, his hands gentle, to protect her ribs and absorb the shock when she would have jolted.

Through it, Rio held her tightly against his mouth, his hard hands digging into her as he held onto her oil coated thighs.

Several long moments later with Clay cuddled against her, soothing her body with long calming strokes, Rio finally lifted his head.

"I love how you taste, sugar. I want the taste of your pussy in my mouth every day."

She expected them to fuck her, and wondered if she could possibly come again.

Her eyes widened when Rio lay down on the other side of her and joined his brother in stroking her still trembling body. She glanced down and saw their erections pushing furiously against their jeans.

Jesse felt as though her bones had melted. Her eyelids felt so heavy that it became an effort to keep them open. When they made no move to take off their jeans despite being hard, Jesse frowned.

"I thought you wanted sex," she murmured sleepily.

"No sex for you until those ribs and that arm are completely healed," Clay told her, the tension in his voice apparent. "We love you, baby." He told her tenderly, kissing her eyelids as they closed. "We want you to feel good and to know how much we care about you."

Rio slid off the bed and went into their bathroom, appearing with a warm washcloth and a towel. "Let's get you cleaned up so you can sleep."

Jesse fell asleep long before they'd finished.

Chapter 13

The next several weeks were the happiest in Jesse's life.

Business at *Indulgences* continued to increase. Word had gotten out and most of the women in town had stopped in to introduce themselves. Jesse and Kelly had samples ready for them and they absolutely loved the products. People from nearby towns came in, those who frequented the other unique shops in Desire seemed just as enthusiastic about the products from *Indulgences.*

Women who shopped in the lingerie store down the street just had to come in to buy the products that would make them smooth and soft and smell terrific to go with their purchases. Even the men who went to Jake's jewelry store to buy collars and nipple rings for their women stopped in. They seemed to love the scents and bought creams and lotions and especially the edible powders and oils for their women.

Some even gave Jesse and Kelly ideas for new products that they had started to work on.

Meanwhile, Kelly glowed, happily not hearing from Simon, and being chased relentlessly by Blade. Jesse had heard from Nat that women had been throwing themselves at him for so long that no one expected him to ever choose one.

According to Rio, the people in Desire found it amusing that Kelly didn't fawn all over Blade and instead had Blade chasing her.

"I really think Blade would be good for Kelly," she'd told him. "He seems so patient most of the time but sometimes he gets this look in his eye like he'd just love to gobble her up. I hope he doesn't lose interest. But right now she's really scared of him, Rio."

"Are you kidding?" Rio had laughed. "Blade's the most patient man I've ever met. This is a challenge to him, darlin'. Blade's on the hunt!"

Jesse went home every night with Clay and Rio. She didn't want to admit that she lived with them, but she slept there every night and little by little everything she owned had been transferred to their house.

They showed her the new house that they had built next door, seeming anxious that she should like it. She loved the house, the open airy feel of it and especially the size of the master bath. All three of them could easily fit in the huge shower and with the multiple spray jets and none of them would be left freezing.

When she asked why they hadn't yet moved into it, they'd explained that they wanted all new things inside and enlisted her help in picking out furniture and decorating it.

They shopped for things for the house over the course of several weeks. They hounded her for her opinion on furniture, bed linens, dishes, curtains, everything. Whatever she chose ended up in the new house.

They would all be moving in as soon as the Preston brothers finished the custom bed they'd ordered.

Jesse stood aside now in the large living room as men carried in a huge television. She glanced up at Clay.

"Do you think it's big enough?"

Clay smiled as he watched the delivery men unwrap it. "Rio and I couldn't resist."

He looked down at her and frowned when he met her eyes. Taking her arm, he led her into the kitchen where they found Rio washing up.

"The new guy's pretty good, really knows his way around horses." Rio paused. "What's wrong?"

"That's what I'm trying to find out." Clay grasped Jesse's chin and lifted her face to his. "What is it, baby?"

"Well, I'm not sure how to say it. I don't want you to get mad."

"What?" Clay demanded.

"You let me pick out all this stuff." In face they had made her pick out everything. Well, except for the television.

When they looked at each other and then back to her she shifted uncomfortably. "Well, actually there are a couple of things bothering me about that." She chewed her bottom lip worriedly as she faced them.

"It's just that I realized how much all this must be costing you. You won't even let me pay for the security system and when I went to ask Lucas how much it cost, he wouldn't tell me."

"Darlin', are you worried about money?" Rio asked, smiling.

"We've been making good money at *Indulgences*. I'd like to help pay for some of the stuff." She threw her good arm out. "After all, I'm staying here free. You won't even let me buy food and I eat here every day."

Clay grinned at her and pulled her to his chest. He bent to touch his lips to hers before straightening.

"Baby, Rio and I have more money then we could spend in ten lifetimes."

Jesse pushed against his chest and leaned back in his grip.

"Listen, I know that you do all right with the ranch and that you live simply, but all this stuff must be really expensive."

Rio leaned in. "God, I adore you," he told her before touching his lips to hers. "They found oil on our property years ago. Money is not a problem. You said something else is bothering you. What is it?"

She felt Clay move in behind her until she found herself once again wedged between them, her favorite place to be. Her nipples hardened against Rio's stomach. Clay's hands felt hot on her hips and she could feel his cock pushing against her back.

Although they pleasured her night after night and sometimes, most of the time, allowed her to pleasure them, they hadn't fully made love with her, no, she reminded herself, had sex with her, since Brian's attack.

She squirmed restlessly in their arms, accidentally bumping Rio with her cast. He jerked back as though burned, grimacing and lowering his forehead to hers.

"What time is your appointment?" Her cast came off today and they all looked forward to the night ahead.

"Two o'clock." Jesse grinned. "I've already picked out what I'm wearing tonight, one of the nighties you bought me before…"

"Excuse me?" A voice came from the living room. Jesse had forgotten the delivery men. "I've got it," Rio told Clay with a glance at Jesse. She tried to look busy folding a towel while she avoided their eyes.

"You don't have to avoid the subject, Jesse," Clay told her softly, lifting her face to his.

"I don't want to talk about it."

"There's nothing that we can't talk about, baby. The only way that this relationship is going to work is if the three of us can talk about whatever is bothering us." He regarded her, his eyes tender. "Rio and I made a huge mistake with you. We fell for you so hard and so fast that when we heard you on the phone it felt like a kick to the gut."

The emotion in his eyes had tears pricking hers.

"We thought that maybe we wanted it so much we misunderstood your feelings. Maybe you didn't feel the same way we did. Maybe we saw what we wanted to believe."

"I'd never felt like that before. Even Brian, in the beginning, never got to me the way that the two of you did."

Rio walked back into the room and glanced at them. "The men are gone."

Clay nodded, his eyes never leaving Jesse's.

"Do you still feel that way?"

Jesse met their piercing gazes. "I'm afraid." She stepped back and Clay seemed reluctant to release her. "It all happened so fast." Jesse swallowed the lump forming in her throat. "I hurt so much when I got married. Little by little I closed off the pain and eventually felt nothing at all."

She idly traced a vein in the granite countertop, avoiding their eyes.

"When I met you, I couldn't help feeling all the things that I had thought I would *never* feel. For the first time in years I felt feminine and beautiful." She closed her eyes against the burn in them. "You both made me feel so wanted and when you held me, I felt warm and safe like nothing could hurt me."

She opened her eyes and felt a tear slide down her cheek.

"One misunderstanding, a lack of trust, and it was all gone. I felt dirty and ugly and helpless," she whispered sadly.

"*No!*" Clay crossed the distance between them in two large strides. Grasping her shoulders he spun her to face him, his face full of misery.

"It's not gone. Rio and I are very much in love with you. I can't imagine what our lives would be now without you in it." His voice lowered, became more tender, a sharp contrast to the turmoil in his eyes.

"I know in my heart that you love us. I know how hard it was for you to let us in. We betrayed that trust, we both know that. Just as we both know it will take time for you to forgive us. But make no mistake, Jesse, this is not and never will be over between us."

Rio moved forward and Jesse saw him shoot a warning glance at Clay. He lifted her onto the counter.

"We went to town once, a few days after we told you to leave. Did you know that?"

Jesse lifted her gaze to his. "No, um, I never saw you around. I thought you'd been avoiding me."

Rio shifted, spreading her thighs and moving between them. "We saw you with a man outside your store. We thought it was your ex husband." He reached up and ran his fingers through her hair.

"He touched your hair."

She heard the anger in his voice and stared up at him in wonder. "But, that was—"

Rio put a finger over her lips to silence her. "We know now that it was Kelly's brother, but we didn't know it then."

Jesse froze in shock as Rio's wrapped his arm around her waist and laid his head on her breast. Her arms automatically moved to comfort him.

"We wanted to kill him, Jesse." His voice sounded muffled against her chest as his arms tightened around her.

Jesse didn't know what to say as she held him against her breast, running her hands through his hair soothingly as she looked over his head to Clay.

The look on his face as he watched her comfort his brother stole her breath. His eyes blazed, burning with love and possessiveness.

"We came home and got drunk," Rio continued as Clay's gaze held Jesse's entranced. "We cursed you and wanted so much to hate you."

Rio lifted his head. "We couldn't."

He lifted a hand to touch her cheek. "We hadn't been back to town since then. We couldn't bear to see you with another man again. The night Brian showed up, Clay and I sat in the bar trying to work up the courage to come to see you, to beg you to come home with us. We ran into Jake and Blade there."

He sighed. "Blade told us what had happened. We were getting ready to run over there when Jake got the call from Kelly."

Rio's eyes shimmered. "I've never been so scared in my life. I was so afraid he would kill you before we could get to you." His expression turned murderous. "I swear to you, if he had, I would have killed him right then. The only reason that he didn't get hurt worse than he did was because you had been hurt and needed us."

Jesse couldn't stand to see her usually playful and mischievous lover look this. Rio looked brokenhearted.

"Please don't," she pleaded.

Clay moved forward and took her hand in his.

"We love you, baby. The house is for you. We want to live here with the woman we chose to be our wife."

Jesse gasped and looked from one to the other incredulously. She watched as Clay took a box from his pocket and opened it, revealing a sparkling ring with two square diamonds side by side.

"Will you wear this, baby? Will you be our wife?"

Jesse looked at the glittering ring. She wanted too much to believe that it would work. But, she had been married before.

Looking from one to the other, seeing the love in their eyes, she wanted nothing more than to say yes.

But their relationship was too new, too fragile. She eyed them sadly.

"I can't," she choked.

She saw the pain flicker in their eyes. They glanced at each other, then back at her.

"Why not, darlin'?" Rio asked softly, running his hands up and down her arms. She watched Clay turn away, scrubbing a hand over his face as he looked down at the ring and closed the box.

"I'm scared," she breathed.

Clay spun and moved back to her.

"What are you afraid of, baby? Rio and I will take care of you. We love you, baby."

The fear and anxiety, the need and the regret made Jesse panic. How could they do this? How could they pressure her like this when they knew she couldn't handle a commitment after all that had happened?

She knew that she loved them. What she had felt with Brian, even when they had first married, paled in comparison to what she felt for Clay and Rio.

If she allowed herself to let go completely, to give all of herself, and they turned her away again, it would break her.

Brian had hurt her until she closed herself off from him. But he had not broken her.

When Clay and Rio sent her away, she hadn't committed herself to even staying here. She'd held herself back.

They wanted it all now. If she gave it all and they broke it off with her again, it would destroy her. How could she trust them not to?

She panicked at the thought of how much they wanted to take care of her, make her dependant on them. She had grown strong, stronger than she had ever believed possible when her relationship with Brian disintegrated.

She'd paid the bills and raised a child single handedly. She took care of Kelly, they'd started a business and she paid for Alex's college without a cent of help from her ex-husband.

She'd learned to be strong. She liked being in control of her life.

Would marriage to Clay and Rio make her weak, dependent?

She felt the fear grow, taking her by the throat, and fear made her angry.

"You say you love me but you don't even know me!" She jumped down from the counter and faced them. "The first time your *love* got tested, it failed."

She skewered a finger into Clay's chest. "If you knew me, you would have known that I'd never betray you." She paced the kitchen angrily. "If you'd loved me, you would have trusted me. If you knew me and cared about my feelings, you'd know that it's important to me to be able to take care of myself and you'd stop trying to wrap me in cotton. You want to make me so dependent and weak that I would only be a shell."

Clay lifted a brow. "So you don't think we know you well enough to be in love with you? If that's true, whose fault is that? You've been holding parts of yourself back from us, Jesse. I don't like it."

When both men stared at her in amusement, her eyes narrowed.

"What's so funny?" she snapped.

"What is it you think we don't know about you, darlin'?" Rio raised a brow and she wanted nothing more than to smack the amused look still on his face.

"I have a temper." She raised her chin defiantly. "It's so bad that Brian always left when I got mad."

Rio grinned. "No kidding."

"Arrrhhhh!" She stomped her foot. "You're not taking this seriously. We're going to have a big fight one day and you're going to decide that I'm too bitchy to put up with. I'm not going to shut up to appease you. When I get mad, I *scream.*"

Clay's lips twitched. "You scream when you come, too." He came closer, running a finger up and down her arm.

"After the number of times we've tasted your passion, we know you must have a temper to go along with it."

Rio's grin widened. "Bring it on, darlin'. You don't really think your temper would put us off, do you? There's nothing as sweet as turning an angry woman's temper into something a lot more fun. Any time you want, you put us to the test. Clay and I love a challenge."

She didn't trust the look of satisfaction on their faces. "We haven't known each other long enough to talk about getting married."

She watched them suspiciously, not trusting the looks on their faces.

Clay raised a brow in challenge. "So before you agree to marry us, you want us to get to know each other better?"

"You may change your mind." Jesse moved to the table and sat, fear making her knees weak. "I can't let you take me over," she whispered. "I can't let you make me so dependent on you that I can no longer take care of myself. I know you've been waiting a long time for someone to share, to take care of."

She took a deep breath and faced them squarely.

"I may not be the one you need."

Clay and Rio glanced at each other, an unspoken message passing between them. They both looked at her tenderly.

"I guess you'll have to find a way to keep us in line." Clay ran a finger lightly down her cheek. "You take care of us every bit as much as we take care of you, just in a different way."

Rio moved in behind her. "It will take a strong woman to handle both of us. A weak woman wouldn't dream of going toe-to-toe with Clay the way you did a few minutes ago. I have a feeling I'm going to get the same if I make you mad."

Rio fisted her hair and moved it aside, exposing the tender column of her neck that they loved to nuzzle. It always turned her to putty.

"A weak woman would bore us to death. We like having a strong woman to love."

He scraped his teeth down her neck. Her eyes closed in ecstasy as thousands of little tingles went through her, arrowing toward her nipples and making them pebble hard.

"I also like finding all your weak spots. A strong woman has strong passions. It makes me feel ten feet tall when I can make you weak with desire, knowing that Clay and I are the only ones who can make you feel this way."

A rush of moisture dampened her panties. Her breath caught. Clay held her in place, his hands on her shoulders firm as he moved closer. His breath felt warm on her hair when he bent forward.

"We'll do it your way, baby. I want you to be sure because there will be no turning back once we get that ring on your finger. But if you want us to know you better, you'd best be prepared to give us your all."

He lifted her chin. "If there's something bothering you, spill it. If you want to yell at us, do it. We'll fight. Lord, will we fight, but then we'll have a hell of a lot of fun making up." He bent down and nipped her bottom lip. "We'll see just how well we know each other when I work my cock up that tight ass of yours and fuck you until you scream."

He pulled her into his arms and lowered his mouth to hers, stealing her breath with a kiss so hot and possessive that her knees buckled.

When he accidentally bumped her cast, he tore his mouth from hers, his eyes glittering darkly.

"Go get that cast off and keep your appointment at the spa." At her startled look, he tweaked her nose playfully. "Yeah, we know about that. We take care of what belong to us. Get used to it."

He stepped back and her hands moved to his chest. "The new bed is being delivered in a little while. Rio and I are going to set it up and put on some of those new sheets you picked out."

When Rio loosened his hold on her hair, she automatically leaned back against his chest as his arms came around her.

She closed her eyes as she leaned back against Rio's chest and ran her hands idly over the muscles in Clay's.

Her eyes opened, though, when Clay grasped her chin.

"We'll start all over." His voice lowered, full of dark promise. "We'll be in our new bed in our new home. You'll soon realize what Rio and I feel for you is real. We know you, baby, probably better than you know yourself. We see in your eyes what you deny. If you think this is only sex, sugar, you're sadly mistaken."

His voice lowered in that way that always drove her wild, melted her inhibitions away.

"Tonight we'll take you the way we've been dying to. Tonight we'll show you what it means to be our woman. Rio will fuck your pussy while I'm shoving my cock in that gorgeous ass of yours. When he pushes in, I'll pull almost all the way out. Then I'll push my cock all the way into your bottom while Rio pulls almost all the way out of your pussy."

The fire in his eyes burned through her. Her panties became drenched just thinking about it. She closed her eyes as he continued.

"There won't be a single moment that one of your lovers isn't pushing into you, you'll be so full, your body will be struggling to stretch to accept us."

He reached down a pinched a nipple, sending her reeling.

"We all know that you're going to feel that ass burn as it's stretched. Your pussy will be on fire as your body struggles to accept the double penetration. And we all know just how much you love that little bite of pain. Don't we, baby?"

"Oh, God," she whimpered.

"What in the hell would we do with a weak woman?" Rio growled in her ear, and swatted her on the bottom as he turned her toward the door.

"Go. We'll be waiting for you. Hurry back, darlin'"

She glanced at Clay and saw his gaze travel over her body. She saw the knowledge of her body's response to his words in his eyes.

"Get ready, baby. Tonight you get all of us. And we get all of you."

Chapter 14

Jesse fidgeted nervously, so excited about the night ahead that she could barely sit still while the intern removed her cast.

The cheap car she'd bought kept stalling on her and she hadn't yet mentioned to Clay or Rio. Before she could get it started, her cell phone rang.

"Did everything go okay with your appointment? Did they have any trouble removing the cast?" Clay asked without preamble.

Jesse laughed. It gave her a warm fuzzy that he cared enough to check on her.

"Of course. Why? Did you think that they would cut my arm off by mistake?"

"For someone who's depending, very much, on my patience a little later, you're not going to want to push it now."

One sentence in that low voice of his and her body jumped to attention. She could almost see the amusement on his face as he teased her.

"I'm really very sorry," she whispered mischievously. "The man who took my cast off seemed *very* nice. He even said that if I took off my clothes he would check the rest of me. When I told him that my breasts felt achy, he offered to massage them and—"

"*What?*" Clay thundered in her ear.

When she giggled, she heard him sigh.

"Careful, baby. You don't want to mess with me right now."

"Mmmm, could that be one of those weak spots Rio talked about earlier?"

He sighed again. "Where you're concerned, baby, I have quite a few of them."

Jesse just melted. 'I have quite a few of them where you and Rio are concerned myself. You two always seem to take advantage of them."

Clay chuckled. "Dealing with you, Rio and I need every advantage we can get. Otherwise you'd walk all over us and God only knows what kind of trouble you'd get into."

"I resent that!"

"No doubt. The bed just got here and Rio and I are going to put it together. Go enjoy yourself with Nat at the spa. Come home right after."

"Or what?" She couldn't resist teasing him.

"Or else that ass of yours is gonna be bright red when I fuck it."

Jesse gasped and tried to think of a reply but he had already disconnected. The stinker.

Nat pulled into the parking lot of the spa right behind her. She loved having the chance to see her sister all the time like this. When Nat moved away all those years ago, her life had gone to hell in a hurry. She'd often wondered if she'd married Brian because of the loneliness she felt without Nat around.

Inside Nat laughed when she told her about the fight she'd had with Clay and Rio.

"You really didn't think your temper would turn them off, did you?"

"It turned Brian off."

Nat wrinkled her nose. "Brian wasn't a real man. Most of the men in this town look forward to a good fight. It keeps it challenging. And no man around here wants a *yes* woman. How boring would that be?"

"You and Jake fight a lot?"

"Absolutely. He likes to get his way all the time. He's overbearing and arrogant and he always wants to do what's *best* for me. I don't always agree."

"But, before you got married, didn't you get afraid that he would try to take you over, that you would become the kind of woman who always said yes?"

"Me?"

"Well, he is bigger and stronger than you."

Nat fluttered her lashes. "He has his strengths, sweetie, and I have mine." She laughed. "He's always saying that he has to constantly be on guard or I would get away with murder."

Jesse looked at her sister in surprise. "Clay just said the same thing to me."

"See?" Nat patted her arm. "They're nothing like Brian, honey. They don't want to pick and choose parts of you that are acceptable, that they can handle and get you to lose the rest. They want the package."

As Jesse and Nat finished their spa treatments, Jesse thought about what her sister had said.

She knew it would take time for her to get used to being involved with someone who had an emotional attachment to something other than money.

To have two men not only accept, but *embrace* everything she threw at them made her head spin.

Jesse returned to the house late in the afternoon. She wouldn't allow herself to think of it as home, at least until she and her men settled things between them.

Walking in the front door, she smiled when she heard voices coming from the kitchen. They both looked up from their tasks when she walked into the room, the welcoming light in their eyes warming her.

Rio turned from his task of setting the table when she walked into his arms and lifted her face for his kiss.

"Mmm, you smell good enough to eat, darlin'."

She smiled and moved to Clay and he kissed her thoroughly. "Mmm," he murmured running his hands under her shirt and up and down her back. "Soft, too. Let me see your arm."

"What's all this?" She spotted several take out cartons on the table.

"We got dinner from the diner. Gracie says 'hi'."

They examined her arm, kissing it all over and sending tingles through her, before they sat down to eat. Jesse's stomach rumbled when she smelled the fried chicken Gracie's men had made.

Rio laughed when he heard it.

"I guess we're going to had to feed you so you have the energy for tonight."

Jesse blushed furiously as they served up the food, making sure that she had everything she wanted before they started on their plates.

How could a woman resist men like these two?

A question that had been plaguing her came back to the surface. It never seemed to be the right time and she didn't want to ruin the mood, to wipe the look of lust and anticipation from her lover's faces.

"What is it, baby?"

Startled, Jesse glanced up to find both men looking at her questioningly. Seeing the concern on their faces replace the joy that had been there only a moment ago, she sighed.

"I didn't want to bring this up now. I know you said that we could talk about anything but maybe now isn't the right time."

"Out with it, Jesse." Clay's tone brooked no argument. "I don't want you thinking about anything tonight except what Rio and I are doing to you."

Jesse rubbed her forehead and cursed herself for letting them see that something bothered her. She'd become very adept at hiding her feelings and uncomfortably aware of how easily Clay and Rio saw right through her.

"That's just another example. You two pay such *attention*."

When they glanced at each other in confusion she almost smiled.

"I just wondered what happened to your marriages. I mean," she gestured wildly, "how can a woman resist a man who notices and actually *cares* about, well, everything about her."

Clay smiled at her mockingly. "You do, consistently."

"That's not true and you know it. Just because I want to be sure before agreeing to get married again doesn't mean I've been able to resist either one of you." She frowned at him. "Don't think I haven't noticed that you've managed to move me into your house and into your bed when I told you that I wanted to stay at the apartment."

When Rio chuckled, she turned on him. "Have I managed even once to say no to either of you when it comes to sex? Don't you think I see that somehow everything I own has been moved here?"

Rio reached for her hand and lifted it to his lips.

"The day you marry us, it's *your* house, *your* bed. That's why you picked out all the furniture and stuff. It's all for you. We live with you, not the other way around."

Before Jesse could think of a reply, Clay interrupted.

"The answer to your question is that neither of us felt the way we should have felt about our wives."

Clay sat back, his dinner apparently forgotten. "I got married because she tricked me into getting pregnant and I was too young and stupid to see it until it was too late. I never loved her and never pretended to."

He leaned forward, his eyes steady as they met hers. "Rio and I always knew we wanted a relationship like our parents had."

"When we first met you told me that your parents lived like us."

Clay nodded. "So did our grandparents. We were born and raised in Desire. Our parents moved here when they got married. When they died, the whole town mourned."

"Why didn't you and Rio share the woman you married?" she blurted.

Clay chuckled and looked at his brother. "Rio couldn't stand to be in the same room as Alicia."

Jesse looked at Rio who shrugged.

"She was a manipulative bitch looking for a meal ticket. When she realized the ranch didn't make the kind of money she wanted, she moved on."

"And you?" Jesse asked Rio. "What happened with your marriage?"

"I settled." Rio sighed. "I gave up when Clay got married and I wanted a family, children. I thought I could grow to love her. I couldn't."

Jesse's heart lurched to see the regret in his eyes.

"At least I know Kyle's mine. After he was born, she fucked every man she could, trying to make me jealous enough to care."

He picked up his glass of iced tea and drank as though trying to wash a bad taste from his mouth.

"It had the opposite effect."

He regarded her hotly. "Now you, on the other hand, would have your bottom spanked until you couldn't sit and would be tied to the bed for a month if you even *thought* about letting anyone else touch you. We're both in love with you and neither of us has ever said that to another woman, even our wives."

"The first time we saw you," Clay began softly, "trying to change that flat tire, Rio and I both got hard as stone the minute we laid eyes on you. By the time we got you into the car alone with us, we shook. We wanted you so badly."

He picked up his fork and resumed eating as he watched her.

"We had just about given up hope of ever finding you. We've had sex with many women since our divorces and not one of those women meant anything to us except temporary relief."

Rio nodded and chuckled. "You make us feel like teenagers again." He sobered. "But it's not just sex, Jesse. We worry about you every time you're out of our sight. We can't wait until you get home from the store because all day all we've done is think about you."

Wanting to lighten the mood and get both of them back to the way they'd been when she got home, she smiled coyly.

"Did you think about me today?"

"Oh, yeah, darlin'"

"Really? Thinking about me getting my cast off or about me being at the spa with Nat, getting my pussy waxed?"

Rio choked and reached for his glass of tea while Clay merely smiled.

"Both actually. We thought about your appointment, which is why I called you, but then you seemed anxious to tease me over the phone, something about finding my weak spots, if I remember correctly."

Rio had recovered and she worried about the glint in his eyes.

"Clay told me that you said something about showing this guy that took off your cast your achy breasts."

"I think," Clay told her, his voice low and seductive, "that you should let us see those *achy* breasts and we'll explore some of those weak spots we talked about."

Jesse had been aroused all day thinking about tonight. The gleam in their eyes as they looked at her heightened her senses.

Her panties felt soaked, her pussy clenching in need. Her clit throbbed and her nipples felt so hard and sensitive that she couldn't stand having her clothing hiding them from her men.

Her skin felt too tight. She felt alive around them in a way she'd never felt before. Her arousal always simmered right below the surface, her body well aware of the ecstasy to be found in their arms.

A look, a word in those dark voices they used, a touch and the need boiled, her inhibitions melting away, knowing they would satisfy her every need. They met every demand her body made with a thoroughness that left her more fulfilled than she ever thought possible.

They made her feel *very* naughty.

Right now she felt very naughty indeed. She couldn't back down from the challenge in their eyes. They wanted to know the real Jesse.

Sometimes she felt very brazen and if it turned them off, she wanted to find out now.

Laying down her fork, she reached for the hem of her shirt and pulled it over her head. Rio's eyes flared and his grin flashed.

"Well, well, very nice." He glanced at Clay. "It looks like Jesse's feeling frisky."

Jesse shifted her eyes to see Clay's reaction to her daring. He gave her his full attention, his body tense, but he made no move to touch her. He leaned back in his chair and waited, his brow arched in challenge.

Jesse saw the surprise on their faces even though they'd covered it quickly. It gave her a heady sense of power that she could surprise them like that. Seeing the challenge and interest in their eyes, she realized they didn't seem to mind when she tried to throw them off balance.

They both appeared to have very good balance.

She wondered what it would take to make them lose it and knew it would be something she would continually strive for.

Raising her hands to her breasts, she cupped them through her bra. She hid a smile when they both shifted in their seats.

"You're playing with fire, baby," Clay warned. His eyes flared as he watched her hands trace the lace trim on her bra but neither of them made a move to touch her.

She lifted her face defiantly and reached for the front closure of her bra. Both Clay and Rio watched her hands intently as she unhooked it, leaving the bra in place over her breasts.

They had seen her breasts countless times, had used their hands and mouths on them over and over and yet they watched now as though mesmerized, anxious for a glimpse of her nipples.

She felt powerful, beautiful and very desired. The feeling washed all inhibitions away. She lowered the straps, glancing coyly at each of them. Slowly she separated the two sides, exposing her breasts to their gaze. Removing the bra completely, she tossed it into Clay's lap.

Being half naked while they remained fully dressed made her feel vulnerable and spiked her arousal even higher.

Clay reached over and circled a nipple, almost, but not quite touching her where she wanted him to. When she tried to shift, to get his touch where she needed it, he removed his hand completely and sat back in his chair.

"Your nipples are hard, like little berries. I'll bet they're just aching to be touched."

When Jesse started to reach up to touch them herself, Clay reached out a hand and stopped her.

"Come here and put one of those sweet berries to my mouth and I'll take care of them for you," he dared.

Jesse smiled at him playfully and stood, hands on her hips and swayed toward him. When she moved close enough, she grabbed handfuls of his hair and drew his mouth to her breasts.

She arched when his tongue flicked at her nipple before drawing it into his mouth. When her knees buckled he pulled her across his lap. Her head fell back over his arm as he lifted her to use his lips and teeth to drive her wild while he stroked and lightly pinched her other nipple.

Fire went through her and she knew Rio watched her reaction to what Clay did to her. She pressed her thighs together against the throb in her clit and felt the trickle of more moisture as her pussy clenched frantically.

Rio leaned across the table and stroked her arm.

"I want my mouth on that pussy."

Desire, sharp and hot went through her at Rio's words. They knew that their talk drove her higher and the way they spoke when preparing her for sex made her abandon all modesty. All she could ever do is respond to their demands which got more and more erotic all the time.

Never knowing what they would do or say next continuously kept her focused on them and what they did to her.

Clay lifted his head and glanced across the table.

"Clear the table, Rio, and you can have your dessert."

Jesse's eyes widened. She watched Rio lick his lips. His eyes alight in anticipation, he stood and hurriedly removed all traces of their dinner from the table.

Clay's eyes stayed on hers as his hand went to the fastening of her jeans. When he lowered his head to kiss her, she grabbed handfuls of his hair until he stilled, looking at her questioningly.

"What is it, baby?"

"You just offered me to Rio for dessert."

"I did. It's only fair since I got to your breasts first. You belong to both of us equally, baby. Remember that."

"I'm not a dessert," she muttered even as her pussy continued to weep.

Clay chuckled. "Of course you are. Our favorite, and we'll never get enough of you."

Rio had finished his chore and sat back at the table, that grin of his flashing.

"Time for my dessert."

Rio helped Clay remove her jeans and panties and settle her on the table. He pulled her toward him until her bottom rested on the edge. Her stomach fluttered when he lifted her thighs over his shoulders.

"Oh, God."

Jesse watched Rio lower his head. She knew what that talented mouth of his could do to her.

At the first flick of his tongue, he took her control.

Clay reached out and fondled her breasts, his eyes both indulgent and fierce as he watched her response to his brother.

"Feel good, baby?"

She felt her orgasm approach. What started as a flutter low in her stomach quickly spread and she came almost immediately under Rio's mouth.

Her moans filled the room.

He gentled his touch, carefully avoiding her clit as he lapped her juices and slowly built her arousal once again.

She forced her eyes open and saw that Clay watched her face.

"You're beautiful, baby."

Clay lowered his mouth to hers, his tongue sweeping possessively inside, reducing her to a quivering bundle of lust. She clung to him when, with a last devastating swipe of his tongue, Rio moved away.

Clay lifted her into his arms, his mouth still on hers.

Rio followed them into the bedroom and her pulse leapt when she heard the rustle of clothes as he undressed.

Clay lifted his head, his eyes glittering. She turned to see that Rio had a similar look on his face as he reached for her.

"Come here, sugar. Let's break in our new bed."

With her in his arms, Rio sat on the side of the bed and lay back until she lay sprawled on his chest. She dimly heard Clay undress as Rio devoured her mouth with his.

His hands moved over her, using the knowledge he had gained of her body to keep her need mounting.

With a growl and a sharp nip, Rio ended the kiss and lifted her to straddle him, the head of his cock at her pussy entrance. Clay wrapped an arm around her waist from behind while Rio gripped her hips.

Her nails dug into Clay's biceps, her cheek against his chest as they lowered her onto Rio's hard length. She felt his cock push into her inch by throbbing inch, stretching her grasping pussy as he filled her.

Tears pricked her eyes. Her hands tightened on Clay and she turned to face Rio.

"I've missed this so much," she whimpered.

Rio's eyes flashed, his hands moving over her thighs.

"I have too, sugar. I've missed being inside you like hell."

She felt Clay's lips on her hair. He always soothed her before entering her as though knowing that her response to them overwhelmed her.

"Now that you're healed we can take you the way we've always wanted. Are you ready to have us both inside you, baby?"

Clay's voice rumbled low and gravelly, almost violent. Jesse shivered. She'd never heard that tone in Clay's voice before and her body responded sharply to the dark intensity of it.

"Yes," she moaned softly. "But I'm scared."

"Do you trust us, honey?"

"I trust both of you. I want both of you."

"Then you'll have both of us."

His voice had lowered even more and sounded like he'd swallowed pieces of glass.

The atmosphere in the room felt much more intense than it had ever been. With a sudden flash of insight, Jesse realized that to them, taking her together would be their way of finally claiming her.

After tonight, there would be no turning back. She would be theirs.

Clay released her and lubed his fingers. With a hand on her back he lowered her to Rio's chest.

Jesse felt Clay's fingers enter her anus. Her breath caught in her throat as he worked the lube thoroughly into her. With Rio's cock filling her pussy, the feeling almost overwhelmed her with its intensity.

She tried to move on Rio's hard length but he held her still.

"Don't move, honey," he groaned harshly.

"I need to move," Jesse groaned. "It feels so good."

When she felt the head of Clay's cock push at her anus, she stilled.

"Hold her, Rio." His voice was barely recognizable. "She's gonna buck."

She felt Rio's arms tighten around her as Clay pushed forward. The head of his cock stretched the tight ring of muscle more than it had ever been stretched when they used the butt plug on her and Jesse jerked in Rio's grasp.

"It burns," she panted.

"Easy, darlin'," Rio soothed, moving a hand comfortingly over her as the other held her firmly in place.

She felt Clay's hands tighten on her ass cheeks as he continued to slowly press forward.

"Christ," he groaned, sounding tortured, "I've never felt anything so tight in my life. I'm not gonna last. Relax, baby. I'll go slow, I promise."

Jesse struggled to adjust to the incredible fullness. Her entire body became no more than her pussy and her ass, every nerve ending in both coming alive like never before.

Clay took her ass, driving deeper with each stroke until he finally had his cock all the way inside her.

Rio loosened his hold on her and together he and Clay established a rhythm.

Having both her pussy and her anus filled ravaged her senses so completely, she could only hold on and go where Rio and Clay took her.

"Oh, God. It's too much. I can't!" Jesse screamed, fearfully fighting against the violent assault on her senses. She shook with the force of it. The orgasm approaching frightened her with its magnitude.

"No! I can't!" she sobbed. "It's too strong!"

"Let go, damn it!" Rio roared as he moved his hand to touch a thumb to her clit, stroking the too sensitive nub with devastating effect.

She exploded, sparks shooting through her as she came violently, her body jerking with the force of it. They held her firmly in place, growling their own releases, driving deep and shooting their hot seed deep inside her which set off another series of explosions.

Jesse collapsed weakly onto Rio's chest, struggling to catch her breath. Strong hands soothed her, deep voices crooned to her until her breathing slowed and her racing heartbeat began to settle.

Even with all they had shared, all that they had done to each other, Jesse hadn't been prepared for what she'd just experienced. When she heard their murmured exclamations of surprise she knew it had stunned them as well.

"Fuck. Am I dead?" Clay groaned.

Rio bit off a choked laugh. "If you are, so am I. And we're in heaven."

Several long minutes later, Jesse felt Clay withdraw from her and press his lips to her back, rubbing a hand tenderly over her bottom.

"Don't move, baby. I'll be right back."

Jesse smiled against Rio's chest.

"I don't think I could move if I had to."

Rio chuckled as he lifted his head and pressed a hard kiss to her lips. Dropping his head back to the bed, he continued to caress her.

"If you think you're ever getting away from us after that darlin', you're crazy."

"It could just be sex. This may not last." Jesse couldn't help protesting. She couldn't commit herself until they came to some sort of understanding. She could feel them gaining power over her more and more every day and it scared her to death.

She felt a warm washcloth moving over her bottom and felt Clay part her cheeks to clean her. She jerked and tried to get up, uncomfortable with such intimacy, but Rio held her firmly in place, withdrawing from her so Clay could finish his task.

"Stay still baby, let me get you cleaned up so you're more comfortable." Clay continued to take care of her thoroughly.

"I can do it myself," Jesse protested. "It's embarrassing."

"Embarrassing? After what we just did?"

Jesse heard the smile in Clay's voice. "I love taking care of you, baby. It shouldn't be embarrassing. I've seen, touched and tasted just about every part of you. Whatever I've missed, I'll get to."

When he finished, he got rid of the washcloth and they settled her in the bed between them.

"I love the new bed." Jesse snuggled deep, her body rapidly cooling.

"At least there's more room than in the other one." Clay settled beside her.

Rio turned to the side and rested his head on his bent arm.

"If you two are done with the small talk, I'd like to get back to what we our discussion, Jesse."

Jesse saw Clay looked over at Rio and frown.

"What's going on?"

"Jesse still thinks it's just sex between us and that what we feel for each other is going to somehow magically go away."

"Oh?" Clay raised a brow.

Jesse avoided their eyes. "I just think we should be sure. I've been through one bad marriage and so have both of you. I would think you'd want to wait, to make sure that I'm really what you want." Her voice broke. "I couldn't handle it if you decided later that we'd all made a big mistake."

"I think you know better," Rio told her as he ran a finger down her arm. "I think we've just proven that we belong together."

"Baby," Clay held her chin, forcing her to look up at him. "Rio and I aren't going anywhere and neither are you. We know what we want and it's you. Take the time you need to settle it in your head. Your heart and your body already know where you belong."

Clay ran his fingers lightly over her cheek and she felt it tingle at his touch.

"You've just recovered from an attack, just opened a business and moved to a new town. And whether you're ready to admit it or not, you moved here because you love us."

He rolled to his back and dropped his head on the pillow.

"Just live here with us, settle in. We'll talk about marriage again when you're ready."

Jesse sighed and shifted. Rio pulled her against his side until her head rested on his chest. He chuckled when Clay grunted.

"You've had her for weeks. It's my turn," Rio told Clay drowsily.

Rio had a point. During the time Jesse wore a cast, she'd slept snuggled next to Clay with her cast resting on his chest. Rio had snuggled her back, his arm warm and heavy on her waist.

Tonight their positions had been reversed. She marveled that they continuously wrapped her in warmth in one way or another, either with their bodies or their caring.

Only the even breathing of her lovers could be heard as they started to drift off to sleep. Jesse struggled to stay awake, wanting the time just to *think.*

She was a control freak, she admitted to herself. She'd had to be. Having the sole responsibility of raising a child, making sure all the bills got paid on time, even starting a business to do it, taking care of Kelly, she'd had to be in control to survive.

Now Clay and Rio expected her to let them take care of her, depend on them to be her strength. She couldn't put aside what she'd become. Her strength defined her.

Although, she admitted to herself, it would be wonderful and comforting to have two men who would be there when she needed a shoulder to lean on.

These two had strong shoulders. But would they always be there or would they be gone when she needed them most? It wouldn't do to count on something that wouldn't be around.

"You're thinking too much, baby." Clay's breath brushed warm on her ear. "Go to sleep. We won't let you go, Jesse. It will all work out."

Jesse stiffened and frowned, which they both reacted to by soothing her with their hands.

How had he known she had been still awake and worried? No one had ever paid such *attention* to her before.

She felt Rio kiss her hair as they continued their stroking, lulling her to sleep.

How the hell could she fight this?

It was her last thought before sleep overtook her.

Chapter 15

Jesse thought about Clay's words over and over as the next several weeks went by. The three of them blended their lives together almost effortlessly.

Of course problems arose. Three strong willed people could be counted on to fight. They'd been mostly minor, though, and the three of them usually made up in the bedroom much to their mutual delight.

Jesse knew, though, that a larger fight loomed on the horizon and Clay and Rio had started to lose their patience with her. They wanted her to let them solve all of her problems for her, butting in when she didn't want them to.

The boutique remained a joy, but with Kelly spending most of her time in the workroom trying to keep up with demand, Jesse mostly ran the store front alone.

When demand grew, Jesse and Kelly started staying after the store closed to work in the back manufacturing and bottling products. She continued to ignore Kelly's attempts to get her to go home.

"Jesse, please go home. Clay and Rio aren't going to like it if you're late again." Kelly busily mixed a batch of bath oil while Jesse used a large mortar and pestle to crush the ingredients to scent it.

"The only way I'm leaving," Jesse told her, "is if you go upstairs and promise not to come back down until we open tomorrow."

"Damn it, Jesse. Let me do this. I have nothing to do tonight. Go home to Clay and Rio."

"If you have nothing to do, why did Blade just pull in?" Jesse gestured toward the window, smiling as Kelly turned bright red and whipped her head around to see Blade park his truck.

They watched as Blade got out of his truck, which he'd parked behind the store, his long strides carrying him quickly to the back door.

"Probably the same reason Rio and I are here."

Jesse whirled to see Rio standing just inside the back room while Clay lounged in the doorway. They'd obviously used their key and come in through the front.

"What are you doing here?" Jesse felt her own cheeks redden.

"We've come to take you home, bodily if necessary." Clay's stance told her he couldn't be swayed.

"I called you to tell you I would be late, didn't I? I have work to do."

Jesse glanced at the back door as Blade came through, his brow raised when he heard Jesse's angry retort.

He didn't say a word, just nodded at Clay and Rio. His eyes lit and his lips twitched when he saw Kelly and her reaction to his presence. Then he just leaned back against the door as though preparing to watch the show.

"You're running yourself ragged, Jesse." Rio stepped toward her, took the mortar and pestle from her and moved it aside so he could take her hands in his.

Irritated that she felt the tingle of awareness travel up her arm and shoot to her nipples, she snapped.

"I have a business to run, damn it! I don't tell you how to run the ranch."

"*We* have a business to run." Kelly frowned at Jesse. "You have to stop taking all the responsibility on your shoulders."

"What are you talking about?" Jesse turned on Kelly. "You've been busting your ass for days trying to keep the shelves stocked. You can't do it by yourself."

"*Neither can you.*" Kelly looked surprised by her own outburst.

From the corner of her eye, Jesse saw Blade lift an elegant brow. She knew he deserved most of the credit for breaking Kelly out of her shell.

"Jesse," Kelly reached over and patted her arm. "We need to hire some help. *Indulgences* is growing so fast that we can't keep up with it by ourselves. Neither one of us will be able to have a life and eventually it's going to affect the business."

Jesse winced at the desperation and worry in Kelly's eyes.

She knew that Clay and Rio watched her intently. They had been very supportive of her need to run her own business but she knew they had become increasingly concerned with how tired and stressed she had become.

"We'll talk about it tomorrow." She didn't want to discuss this in front of them. She and Kelly would work it out somehow.

She turned to Blade. "Hello, Blade. Do you and Kelly have a date tonight?"

"Jesse!" Kelly hissed at her. "There's nothing like that between Blade and me."

"Oh?" Blade asked softly. Dressed all in black, he looked like every woman's darkest fantasy.

By the look on Kelly's face, she'd had a few of those fantasies herself.

Blade noticed, of course. Jesse knew those blue eyes of his never missed even the slightest nuances of a woman's response and only a blind man could have missed Kelly's.

"If you ladies are done for the day, I thought I'd take Kelly to dinner." Blade's eyes never left Kelly's flushed face. "You all, of course, are welcome to join us."

"Another time, thanks," Clay continued to watch Jesse from where he stood, still leaning against the doorway.

"Kelly." Jesse ignored the looks both Clay and Rio gave her as she moved around the table to the younger woman. "Go have dinner with Blade. I'll be leaving here soon."

She moved away to pull more ingredients from a cabinet. "We'll talk tomorrow."

Blade walked Kelly out, frowning when she avoided his attempt to take her arm.

Jesse risked a glance at her lovers, not at all surprised to see that they watched her with *the look,* as she called it.

Whenever they had that particular look on their faces she knew that it would be impossible to sway them from whatever they'd decided.

The indulgent tenderness usually glimmering in their eyes when they looked at her had disappeared as their gazes followed her around the workroom. She didn't feel up to arguing tonight and wanted some time to finish the bath oil so she could leave.

"Why don't you two go home? I promise I'll be home in a little while." Jesse added the ingredients she'd crushed to the large pot and stirred.

When she turned to get the other ingredients from the table, she ran straight into Clay's hard chest. He stood directly behind her and she hadn't even heard him move.

She looked up at him resigned, but unsurprised to see that he still wore *the look.*

"I have work to finish," she told him firmly.

"No, you don't. You're coming home with us. Now."

"But I'm not finished." With her hands on her hips, she faced both of them. "Do not try to tell me how to run my business."

"I'm not trying to tell you how to run your damned business!" Clay roared, grabbing her shoulders. "You're wearing yourself out, trying to do everything." He swore under his breath. "You clean the house so much that the cleaning woman has nothing to do. You've worked so hard to build this business that you can no longer keep up with it and you'd rather work until you drop before hiring people to help you. You insist on paying for Alex's college with no help from us when we could pay for it easily."

Clay shook her, his patience at an end. "No more! Do you hear me?" He shook his finger at her. "We've tried to let you do what you wanted, but you're not alone anymore."

Jesse met Clay's temper with her own.

"That doesn't give you the right to tell me what to do!"

"It does when you're not taking care of yourself," Clay shouted back.

His voice lowered dangerously. "Don't push me on this, Jesse. You're not going to win."

"Not going to win?" Jesse screeched. "How I run my business and my life is none of your business."

"Oh, Jesse. On that you are very wrong." Clay's eyes glittered coldly.

"If you think I would marry someone who wants to take over my life, *you* are very wrong," Jesse shouted.

"I will, we will, take care of you whether you like it or not. Neither of us will allow you to work yourself to death or make yourself sick with worry, married or not," Clay shouted back. "You're exhausted, worried and stressed. Do you really think we're just going to stand by and watch you do this to yourself?"

Before Jesse could respond, Rio nudged Clay aside. A look she couldn't decipher passed between them and Clay turned away, moving to stand at the window.

Rio grasped Jesse's hands in his and held them against his chest.

"Edna, the woman who's taken care of our house for years is very proud. She's been coming to the house twice a week since our divorces to clean and cook for us. She works for the Rosses and the Jacksons, too.

"Edna has been a widow for years and depends on the money she makes cleaning houses to raise her two daughters. Several of us have tried to give her money but she won't accept charity. Sound familiar?"

His lips thinned. "Edna sees cleaning a clean house as charity. She won't accept our money for cleaning when it's so obviously not needed."

Jesse sighed and gestured to where Clay stood by the window.

"Why didn't he just tell me that instead of being a bully and yelling at me? He's always so quiet and calm with everyone else. The only person he yells at is me."

"And me," Rio nodded. "Or anyone who threatens either of us in any way. What does that tell you, Jesse?"

His lips touched her forehead. "Only you and I can make him crazy with worry. Only you and my brother can make me shake in fear for you. We belong together, Jesse."

Damn him. She couldn't let him sweet talk her into agreeing to anything she couldn't be sure about. Pulling her hands from his grasp, she moved away before he could weaken her further.

"Fine, if Edna has been working for you, I don't want to interfere, especially if she needs the job."

She looked up from beneath her lashes.

"It would help a lot, not to have to deal with cleaning the house." She slid a glance at Clay. "It'll give me more time to catch up on things here."

"Careful," Clay warned without turning.

"Jesse," Rio sighed. "There are probably several people in town who could use a job, honey."

Rio moved closer and the heat from his body and his clean scent wrapped around her.

"The people in this town take care of each other, Jesse." Rio lifted her chin, his tone serious. She'd found that both he and Clay took the problems of the people in town very seriously.

"You had no problem moving here and opening a business because you had family already here, people that everyone knows and respects."

He touched her arm. "We don't readily accept outsiders here, Jesse. It's fine for people to come to town to do business, as long as they cause no trouble. But, we're very careful about who lives here and who operates businesses here."

He glanced at Clay who had turned from the window to watch Jesse, but remained quiet.

"The people in Desire choose to live their lives in a way that others may criticize. We welcome those who accept our way of life even if they don't choose to live it. We won't tolerate people confronting our women on the street and making insulting remarks to them about how they choose to live."

Jesse frowned. "People have insulted women who live here?" At Rio's grim nod, she asked. "Do they insult the men, too?"

Clay's lips twitched. "They're not brave enough to say anything to any of the men and too stupid to realize that insulting the women is much worse."

Clay shrugged. "Once they do, they're no longer welcome in Desire and are forced to leave."

"Forced? Forced how?" Jesse started to realize just how little she knew about the town she now called home.

"Depends," Clay shrugged again. "For someone like your ex-husband, who actually attacked you, well, whoever sees him around town will call us and keep an eye on him until we can get to him. Then we would do to him what he did to you, escort him out of town and makes sure he understands not to ever come back."

Jesse gulped. Jeez, he wasn't kidding. She looked at Rio for confirmation, her eyes widening as he nodded gravely.

"For an insult, nothing quite so dramatic," Rio told her. "but just as effective.

"Like what?" Jesse asked guardedly.

Rio crossed his arms over his chest. "A man lived here about five or six years ago. He seemed nice to everyone, but we all suspected he beat on his wife, although she would never admit it. He ran a little ice cream store. He did a good business until one day he made the mistake of asking Gracie how she had the nerve to show her face in church every Sunday when she fucked three men."

Jesse gasped, appalled. Gracie loved her three husbands so much and they absolutely adored her. She couldn't believe that anyone would say such a thing to her.

She could see the remembered anger on both Clay and Rio's faces.

"What happened to him?"

Rio smirked. "Everyone in town lost their taste for ice cream. No longer welcome in any of the stores, he had to leave town to buy food or gas. He and his family left within a month."

"Good." Jesse nodded, glad that everyone had stood behind Gracie and that the man hadn't gotten away with talking to her like that.

"So," Rio continued, "since you have a business and could use the help, hiring someone from here who needs a job would be a great way to repay the town for welcoming your business here."

Jesse massaged her forehead where she felt the beginning of a headache.

"You're right. Hiring someone from town would help us and give someone a job who could really use it."

At his satisfied look, she shook her head in amusement.

"I can't believe you've talked me into not only Edna, but hiring help. I'll bet you've been talking unsuspecting females out of their panties your whole life."

"Don't laugh, darlin'. I talk you out of yours all the time."

Jesse sucked in a breath. That grin of his really should be outlawed.

"Are you ready to go home now?"

"Yes, I just have to lock up."

As Jesse began turning off the lights and the men locked the doors and windows, she thought about the day Brian showed up.

"Did you ever find out from the sheriff who Brian cheated?" She looked at both men curiously. "I asked him myself but he said he didn't know anything yet and would be talking to the two of you."

"No, baby." Clay checked the locks on the windows while Jesse put things away.

"Your ex-husband wouldn't even admit he'd cheated anyone. Ace couldn't get anything out of him before the state police came to pick him up."

Rio came back from checking that the front had been secured.

"We're keeping an eye on Simon, though. We all know what he looks like." He grinned in anticipation. "We're ready for him if he ever decides to show up."

"No," Jesse shook her head. "I don't want either of you involved."

Rio turned from where he sniffed the contents of the large pot.

"Excuse me?" She saw that Clay had once again tensed and turned to face her.

"Kelly's my responsibility. She came here because I asked her to. I can handle Simon. I have before."

Rio's eyes glittered angrily and Clay's looked even colder than before.

"It's not up to you to handle Simon. You stay clear of him. Do you understand?" Rio smashed a fist on the table making the bottles jump.

Where Clay's icy temper froze her, Rio's burned hot.

"You are under *our* protection. Until Blade claims Kelly and she accepts, she's ours to protect, too."

"Then I'll just move back here," Jesse retorted angrily.

"You'd still have our protection and Jake's as well. You're his wife's baby sister and his responsibility if you're not claimed, which you have been. He'll always watch out for you just as we will with Kelly but you accepted our claim. You moved in with us."

Rio moved closer until his nose almost touched hers.

"You knew the rules of this relationship and the way we live in this town before you took us on, darlin'. I don't give a fuck who or what you *think* you can handle."

His voice lowered. "If you even attempt to try to face him alone, I'm going to turn you over my knee and spank those ass cheeks until I cool down enough to deal with you."

"Deal with me?" Jesse cried indignantly. "I'm not a child! And I'm tired of you threatening to spank me whenever I do something you don't agree with!"

"It's not a threat, darlin'," Rio snarled. "It's a promise, one that I'll take great pleasure in keeping."

Clay's voice came from across the room, casual on the surface but so cold it threatened to freeze her where she stood, "Do you really believe that we would allow you to deal with Simon?"

"Allow?" Jesse asked incredulously.

"Yes, allow." Clay dipped his head. "When it comes to your safety and well being, Rio and I are in charge."

His words stung like icy daggers striking her. She'd rather deal with Rio's hot temper than Clay's icy one.

"Do you think," Clay continued, "that we'd let him or anyone else cause you harm? Do you think we'd allow you to put yourself in danger? You belong to us. When it comes to your safety and well being, you'll do as you're told."

He'd moved closer to her, then, grasping her chin, forced her to meet his eyes.

"I'm bigger. I can make you."

"You can't tell me what to do." Jesse tried unsuccessfully to jerk out of his grasp.

"Do you like that little dream world you're livin' in, darlin'?" Rio asked sarcastically from somewhere behind her but she couldn't escape from Clay's firm hold to face him.

Jesse had a sinking feeling in the pit of her stomach. She couldn't let them get away with this. Once she did, they would find something else she couldn't do. Little by little the list would grow until she couldn't do anything.

What if they decided that running a business made her too tired? That the trip to go shopping in Tulsa was too far for her to go? That she couldn't be friends with someone they didn't like.

No, she had to keep her independence and make them understand.

Terrified that this was the moment she'd been dreading, that this had become the beginning of the end of their relationship she faced Clay squarely.

"It means so much to me that you want to protect me," she began. Her eyes stayed steady on Clay's and she caressed the hand holding her chin.

"Good," Clay ran his thumb over her bottom lip before pressing his own to them.

Releasing her chin, he held out his hand to her, apparently satisfied that he'd won their argument.

"Come on, baby. Let's go home."

"Let me finish." Jesse wanted to stomp her foot in frustration.

"I'm glad you care about me enough to want to protect me," she began again. "If I need your help, I'll ask. But I don't need you to shield me. I promise to let you know if I ever need your help. But, I am perfectly capable of taking care of myself."

She watched them both steadily. "It's who I've become. It's who I am now. Will you be able to love what I've become? Will you respect the fact that I need to be able to take care of myself?"

Clay's eyes never left Jesse's. He wanted to be angry. She tried desperately not to let him see her fear, but knowing her, loving her as he did, he could see her terror.

"I know exactly what kind of woman you are, Jesse. I'm not a kid who doesn't know what he wants or what his woman is about." He struggled to keep his tone even.

Despite the fact that she wore that cool mask she still donned whenever she felt the need to protect herself, he could see nothing but fear and raw nerves as she faced them.

"I know that you're strong, independent and usually able to take care of yourself. But there are things that even you can't handle and that Rio and I would happily handle for you, if you let us."

He wanted nothing more than to go to her, wrap his arms around her and hold her until the love usually shining from them when she looked at him replaced the fear.

He wondered how she didn't know they could see it. His eyes stayed locked on hers.

"I wonder if you know the men you've gotten involved with. We're men, Jesse, not lazy spineless boys like your ex-husband. We'll be your shield, always, Jesse. That's the kind of men we are, what kind of men we'll always be. We'll protect you from everything we can, even yourself."

He opened the door, grasping her arm lightly as she moved to go past until she looked up at him. "We're going to fight, Jesse. Our need to protect you, to take care of you is just as strong, if not stronger than your need to be independent."

Clay glanced at Rio and saw that his brother watched Jesse hungrily. They both knew she was the perfect woman for them but first she had to accept who they were.

"I'll never forgive myself for not being around when Brian attacked you. That will never be allowed to happen again. Anyone wanting to hurt you will have to go through us to do it. That won't be easy."

His eyes held hers, letting her see the love he felt for her, his own vulnerability.

"Can you love men like us, Jesse? Can you love men who want nothing more than to love and care for you? Can you respect *our* need to protect you?"

He ushered her out the door and to his truck. Once they all settled, he started the engine and stared out the windshield.

"Maybe you need to think about that, baby, because we can't change the way we are, even for you."

Chapter 16

They brought her home and headed straight for the bedroom. She followed, nervous after the silent ride home. When she saw them throwing a change of clothing into a duffel bag, her heart sank.

"Are you leaving?" she asked tremulously.

Both turned to her; Rio looked impatient while Clay eyed her coolly.

"We'll be at the club for a while. If you need us, call one of our cells."

He zipped the bag closed and straightened.

"We'll sleep at the old house tonight. Take tonight to think about what you want, but know this—I know you and I decided a while ago to accept all that you are, even your temper and strong independent streak, which can both be a pain in the ass."

He held her gaze and she could see how difficult this was for him.

"I guess it's up to you to decide if you can accept all that we are."

He picked up the bag and strode toward her, leaning down to press a hard kiss to her trembling lips.

"Good night, baby."

He walked out without a backward glance.

Jesse turned to Rio.

"I feel the same, Jesse."

He closed the distance between them and ran a hand lightly over her hair.

"We'll fight, we'll make up. We'll drive you just as crazy as you make us. You'll have to put up with us taking care of you the same way you take care of us."

He leaned in to kiss her tenderly, his lips feather light on hers.

"You take care of us in so many ways and don't even realize it. And we love it. Accept us, love us the way we are, Jesse, just as we accept and love everything you are."

He touched his lips to hers again.

"Don't forget to set the alarm. We'll see you in the morning."

With a last quick glance at her he left to join his brother.

An hour later Jesse still paced the house restlessly. The silence in the spacious ranch house scraped her nerves raw. After living with Clay and Rio for the past several weeks, she couldn't take any more of the silence and she called her sister.

"Nat, can you meet me somewhere? I really need to talk to you."

"Sure, honey. What's wrong?"

Jesse sighed, rubbing her churning stomach.

"Clay and Rio left me alone tonight to think about some things. Things I want to talk to you about, but if you're busy—"

"No, I'll meet you at the hotel. We'll have a nice dinner, just the two of us and we'll talk about it. A half hour okay?"

"Sure. Thanks, Nat." She cleared her throat as tears threatened.

"It sure is nice living close to you again. I've missed you."

"Me too, honey, very much. I'll see you at the hotel."

Since the hotel sat next to the club, Jesse couldn't help but search for Clay's truck in the club's parking lot, unsurprised to see it there. They always did what they said they would.

She pulled into the hotel parking lot, amazed to see that even though the parking lot looked pretty full, most of the parking spaces in front of the restaurant remained empty. She wondered why no one had parked there and if it would be all right if she did.

Then she saw the sign.

Reserved for Women

Jesse pulled into one of the spaces and just sat and stared at the sign in amazement.

The owners had reserved these spaces so that the women who came here without a man wouldn't have to walk across a parking lot alone.

It appeared that Clay and Rio didn't stand alone in their determination to protect the women. It showed the level of respect this town's men had for their women. These surprising and amazing men traveled in two very different worlds, somehow blending them into the best of both. They accepted the woman for themselves and tried to support them.

From what she'd seen, the women appeared to be very much in love with their husbands, who did whatever they could to keep their wives happy.

She knew the men could be completely chauvinistic when it came to their women's safety and completely overprotective and unapologetic for putting their foot down when it came to protecting the women.

They lived a very progressive lifestyle with old fashioned values.

After all the arguments with Clay and Rio, all the soul searching she had done, this stupid sign clicked everything into place for her.

Reserved for Women

The best of both worlds.

She wanted to call them, to ask them to meet her at home when Nat pulled into the space next to hers. Her phone call could wait. She needed to talk to Nat.

* * * *

Dinner alone with her sister calmed her even more. Jesse told Nat what had happened with Clay and Rio and how the sign out front had been her revelation.

They each had a glass of wine with their dinner of filet medallions cooked to perfection.

Jesse sat across from Nat feeling as if a huge weight had been lifted off her shoulders. She knew she'd made the right decision and couldn't wait to marry Clay and Rio and begin their new lives together.

"So it looks like you'll be getting married." Nat smiled happily at her sister. "I know you'll be happy with them. Clay and Rio are going to spoil you which is something you never had with that idiot you finally divorced. And I know how happy you make both of them." Nat sighed. "They've been so lonely for so long." She sipped her wine. "Their wives never made them happy. And no one liked either of them. Everybody loves you."

"Everybody loves *you*," Jesse laughed. She reached over to touch her sister's arm.

"I know the reason everyone welcomed me the way they did is because they love and respect you and Jake so much."

"We're all very close knit here." Nat paused to wave at someone who'd walked in. Turning back to Jesse, she leaned forward.

"Sometimes they can drive you crazy, the men I mean, but I've never met a group of men so, I guess *intent* is the best word, on their women." Nat grinned mischievously. "I imagine you've found out how serious they are about satisfying their women sexually."

"It's unbelievable," Jesse giggled. "I thought that kind of mind-blowing sex happened only in erotic novels."

"Nothing like great sex to keep a woman happy." Nat teased and lifted her glass.

Jesse touched her own to it. "Amen to that!"

"Good evening, ladies."

Jesse looked up to see a tall blond man standing next to their table.

"Hello, Ethan," Nat greeted warmly. "Jesse, Ethan Sullivan. Ethan, my sister Jesse Tyler, soon to be Erickson."

"Nat!" Jesse hissed.

Nat ignored her. "Jesse, Ethan and his partner Brandon own the hotel."

Jesse found her hand engulfed in Ethan's.

"Partner?" Jesse asked, remembering Ryder from the garage and his 'partner' Dillon.

Ethan smiled in a way she knew would make women weak in the knees.

"Yes, partner. In every way," he added erotically, chuckling when she blushed. "So I finally meet the woman who has Clay and Rio so tied up in knots." He lifted her hand to his lips. "A pleasure."

His eyes twinkled. "We've waited a long time to see them happy. You must be quite a woman."

Jesse blushed again. "I'm afraid I'm very ordinary."

"Modest, too." Ethan grinned. "Are you ladies having a good time?"

"Absolutely." Jesse smiled at him. "We had a wonderful dinner, sort of a girl's night out."

"So that's why Clay, Rio and Jake are at the club. The three of them are hardly ever there anymore."

"Jake's there, too?" Jesse looked at Nat.

"Yes," Nat laughed softly. "Rio called him right after you called me, something about a poker game."

Her eyes gleamed. "Jake said Rio sounded a little distracted. I wonder why."

"I should call them," Jesse told Nat guiltily. "I don't want them to have to wait until morning for my answer."

"Make them suffer a little longer." Ethan smiled disarmingly. "If they're distracted, I may finally be able to win some money from them. Besides, I hear you've got that beautiful new house all to yourself tonight. Enjoy it. The way those two are with you, I don't think you'll often have a chance to be there alone again."

"Please don't say anything to them. I want to tell them myself." Jesse turned to Ethan.

When Ethan walked away a short time later, Nat turned to her and shrugged. "Ethan will tell them. He won't want them to worry." Nat shrugged. "The men will never keep a secret about the women from each other." She waved a hand dismissively.

"So when can we shop for a wedding gown?"

"And a gown for you. You are going to be my matron of honor, aren't you?"

Jesse saw the shimmer of tears in Nat's eyes.

"Nothing would make me happier," Nat told her tearfully, then smiled. "Let's go Saturday. I don't think Clay or Rio will want to wait long."

Jesse giggled happily. A warm glow filled her knowing that she would soon be married to two men she loved more than she thought possible.

* * * *

Jesse drove up the private road toward what had become her home and when the driveway forked, she glanced toward the old house. With no lights on, she could barely see it. She knew that the men were still at the club, hopefully just playing poker.

She'd had a few uncomfortable moments when she'd realized what else they could be doing there but Nat quickly reassured her.

"There's no way either of them would touch another woman. They've both claimed you and until you tell then you're finished with them, they'd consider themselves taken."

Jesse walked into the new house determined that the old one would remain dark tonight. She wanted them both here with her but first she wanted to get ready.

Remembering Rio's warning, she reset the alarm before heading for the kitchen to pour herself a glass of wine to take with her to the bath.

She walked down the hall, giddy with happiness. She hummed to herself as she danced into the large master bath and began filling the oversized tub, adding a generous amount of peach scented bath salts.

Still humming, she glided back to the bedroom and into the large walk-in closet Clay and Rio had insisted she have to herself while they shared the other.

Just another example, she thought to herself, of how they cared for her.

She sorted through her rapidly growing collection of lingerie, finally settling on a peach gown with strategically placed lace insets. Neither of her men had seen this particular one and she wanted to wear something special tonight.

She reached up to pull the matching robe from its hangar, looking forward to the men's reaction when they saw her in it. She strolled back to check on her bath. Steam rose, scenting the air with the peach scent she loved so much. She turned the water off and smiled. Clay and Rio seemed to love it now, too.

Holding the gown in front of her, she looked in the mirror, swaying as she watched how the material moved fluidly around her.

She carefully laid the gown and robe across the padded bench the men had bought for her. Her body tingled as she remembered some of the more inventive uses Clay and Rio had found for it.

She paused in the act of undressing when her cell phone rang. She looked at the display, grinning when she looked at the display.

"Hello, Rio. Do you miss me? I was going to call you after my bath."

"Were you?"

He sounded distracted. She heard Clay's voice in the background.

She frowned. He sounded angry, but she couldn't make out what he said.

"Rio, what's wrong? Are you and Clay mad at me?"

"No, darlin'. Listen, I want you to go into the master bathroom and lock the door. Stay on the phone with me, darlin'."

"Rio, what's going on?"

"Are you in the bathroom?"

"Yes, Rio.."

"Is the door locked?"

Jesse hurriedly locked the door.

"Yes, I'm in the bathroom with the door locked. Now, what's going on?"

"She's locked in," she heard Rio tell someone, she assumed Clay.

"*Rio!* What's going on?"

"Jesse, someone's on the property. Don't worry, whoever it is isn't in the house yet."

"What?" Jesse gripped the phone tighter. "Someone's trying to break into the house?"

Jesse could hear Clay shout in the background.

"Tell her we're almost there, damn it!"

"Jesse, we're—"

"I heard Clay. How do you know someone's here?"

"We'll explain when we get there. Just stay where you are, darlin'. Keep the door locked."

She could hear the fear and anger in his voice that she could tell he tried to hide from her.

"I set the alarm," Jesse said to herself, but Rio heard.

"I know, darlin'. The sensors outside were activated when you set the alarm. Someone tripped them a few minutes ago."

She heard him reply to something Clay said.

"If someone breaks into the house, won't the alarm sound?" Jesse asked, trying to see out the bathroom window.

"Yes. It's really loud and will probably scare them off. No matter what you hear, you stay locked in the bathroom until one of us comes to get you. Do you hear me? *You stay where you are!*"

Jesse moved to the light switch. Plunging the room into darkness, she moved back to the window. She inched the curtain aside until she could see the back of the property.

Now she could see better and hopefully whoever lurked out there wouldn't be able to see her.

"I don't see anyone out back. I'm going to go see if I can see anything out front."

"No, damn it. Stay there. Clay and I are pulling in now."

She heard several long seconds of muffled cursing.

Suddenly the alarm sounded, blocking out their voices.

Jesse froze. Had the alarm scared the intruder away or had someone entered their house?

The intruder had probably fled. Clay and Rio are here, she reminded herself. They would search the house, find it empty, and come get her.

She just wished they'd turn off the screaming alarm. When it suddenly went silent, she glanced at the door. The sudden dead silence disconcerted her after the wail of the alarm. Moving to the door she strained to hear something, anything.

The sound of a gunshot broke the silence. Jesse jumped in horror.

Had Clay or Rio retrieved their guns from their office or had the intruder fired? Either way it meant that someone was in the house.

She heard sounds like a scuffle taking place followed by a loud crash.

Fear for her men had her clumsily unlocking the door and racing out of the bathroom. If something happened to either of them she didn't think she could bear it.

She raced down the hall toward the sound of Rio's angry curses, coming from the kitchen.

"Jesse! No!"

She heard Clay's angry roar as a hand shot out and grabbed her. The intruder pulled her in front of him to use her as a shield. She saw the glint of a knife as it moved toward her throat. She absently recognized it as one she kept in a block on the kitchen counter.

"Stay back or I'll cut her."

Jesse froze in fear as the menacing voice next to her ear stopped both Clay and Rio in their tracks.

She saw the fear and frustration in their eyes as they watched the intruder caress her throat threateningly with the knife.

Jesse could see that Rio had been hurt, his sleeve red with blood.

The table had been broken, chairs scattered around the kitchen and glass everywhere. Jesse could see that the French doors hung drunkenly, most of the glass gone.

She met Clay's eyes and she wanted to look away from the overwhelming horror she saw in them.

* * * *

Clay felt as though he'd stepped into a nightmare.

He and his brother had been playing poker at the club, anxious about their conversation with Jesse. Jake and Blade sat with them.

When Ethan showed up to tell them that he'd seen Nat and Jesse at the hotel restaurant and that it looked like Jesse would be accepting their proposal, the tension simply drained away.

"She begged me not to tell you," Ethan had told them. "I only came here to tell you because I felt sorry for both of you. You'd probably lose all your money to these two because you're distracted." He grinned at his friends. "I want you to lose it to me. Anyway, as I walked away, I heard them talking about shopping for a wedding dress."

"Thank God!" Rio took a healthy swallow of his whiskey. "But if we're not supposed to know, we have to wait for her to call."

He frowned. "You don't think she'll make us wait till morning, do you?"

Jake, Blade and Ethan had roared with laughter.

The game continued with Clay and Rio looking at their watches every few minutes.

When their remote alarm had sounded, they'd looked at each other in shock and run out of the club without a backward glance even when they heard the other three race out behind them.

Arriving at the house, Blade and Ethan had split up to circle the house while Clay and Rio went in through the front. Jake had stayed in his truck, talking on the phone to Ace.

Before they could get the front door unlocked, the guy had crashed through the French doors in the back, apparently knowing they had pulled in and tried to get to Jesse before they did.

Rio raced into the house, leaving Clay to silence the ear splitting alarm.

He had already moved into the kitchen when he heard the crash. Rio had thrown the intruder onto the kitchen table which broke under the impact.

The young punk had come to his feet with a gun in his hand and fired, hitting Rio in the arm.

Clay dove for the gun, knocking it out of the guy's hand and sending it flying. He'd rolled to his feet to give chase when the guy grabbed a knife from the counter and Jesse raced into the room.

Fear and rage like he'd never known threatened to consume him. He, who, because of his parents deaths while still in his teens, had learned to take control, remain level headed at all times, be calm and cool, even cold, in a crisis, felt almost paralyzed with fear at the threat to Jesse.

"Tell your friends outside to come in," the guy holding Jesse told Clay.

Clay didn't like the wild look in the man's eyes or the way he shook so hard with the knife at Jesse's throat. One slip and Jesse could be gone. He felt powerless to help Jesse as long as this bastard had a knife to her throat and his attention remained focused on him and Rio.

He'd hoped the guy hadn't known about the others. He knew that one of them would distract the guy long enough for Clay to take him.

Right now it looked to be his only chance.

"What friends?"

"Don't fuck with me!" I saw those two looking outside for me. I was on the side when you pulled up and I saw them trying to circle the house to catch me. That's why I had to break in the back!"

His hold on Jesse tightened. "I knew if I got to her before you did, you'd give me what I want to get her back. Call them. Now. Or I swear I'll cut her."

Clay realized the guy only knew about Blade and Ethan. He didn't know about Jake.

He watched as the bastard moved the knife down Jesse's neck toward her breast until her got to her nipple.

"Maybe I'll cut off little pieces of her until I get what I want."

When he pricked her breast with the knife point, Jesse whimpered.

"No!" Clay and Rio both shouted. Blade and Ethan rushed through the broken French door.

"We're here. Don't hurt her." Blade stopped behind Clay, Ethan right beside him.

"Whatever you want, it's yours, just don't hurt her." Clay forced himself to speak calmly when he wanted nothing more than to kill the man with his bare hands.

He'd moved the knife back to Jesse's throat. He looked scared, desperate to find himself in this situation. His attempt to kidnap Jesse had been thwarted and it made him nervous. His hands shook so hard that Clay feared he would cut Jesse by accident.

"I want my fucking money," the smaller man raged. "The money that her husband stole from me. I want it back."

"Ex-husband," Jesse corrected him.

"Shut up, bitch."

The man shook with anger, inadvertently nicking Jesse's throat with the knife.

Clay felt his stomach drop when he saw the trickle of blood on Jesse's neck.

"Calm down. I'll give you the money." Clay's voice lowered as he met Jesse's eyes warningly.

She was going over his knee for this. If she'd stayed put, like she'd been told, she wouldn't be in danger. Now she provoked the man holding a knife to her throat.

"I want one hundred thousand dollars. I know you have it. I checked you out."

"You're right," Clay's kept his voice low and reassuring. "I'll get it for you. Let her go. You don't want to hurt her."

"I want my money and she stays with me until I get it. She's leaving with me. You'll get her back when I have my money." He smiled sickeningly at Clay. "After I've had some fun with her first."

Clay's stomach clenched. This guy wouldn't be taking his woman anywhere.

Jake had no way to get to this guy as long as he kept his back to the wall. Clay knew he had to get him to move. He had no doubt Jake listened to every word and would react accordingly.

"Why don't we go into my office and I'll transfer the money to your account. Just give me the number."

"I don't have a fucking account. Brian stole it all. No, I'm leaving and taking her with me."

"I'm not going anywhere with you, asshole," Jesse growled. "You're just a puny little boy. My fiancées' will break you in half for threatening me."

"Jesse, shut the fuck up." Rio's eyes flashed.

Clay looked at Jesse incredulously. Oh, yes, definitely over his knee. He couldn't let her see the pride he felt at her refusal to be a victim. He never would. His priority had to be her safety and provoking a lunatic with a knife to her throat was not safe.

"I can't let you take her." Clay's voice lowered. "I understand Brian cheated you, but she had nothing to do with it."

"*It's all her fault.*" Spittle shot out of the guy's mouth. "He got arrested because of her. He can't pay me from jail!"

The guy started pulling Jesse toward the doorway. "Enough of this. I'm taking her with me. Get my money. I'll call you tomorrow to tell you where I want you to drop it off. Then you can have her back."

Ethan and Blade had been inching forward, and Clay knew they'd hoped to get close enough to help him if he got the chance to move on the guy. Ethan deftly tied a towel to Rio's arm to stop the bleeding while Blade edged closer.

"Stay back! All of you!"

Jesse gasped when the knife pricked her again.

"If you cut me again I'm going to kick your balls into your throat."

"Jesse," Clay murmured warningly.

"We'll see how tough you are, bitch, when you're tied up and naked. You'll be begging me to be nice to you."

Clay wanted to smash his fist into the sneer on the man's face. The thought of his woman tied, naked, in this man's clutches enraged him.

The guy's wild eyes darted around the room as he backed toward the kitchen doorway.

"Everybody stay where you are. You'll get her back when I get my money."

Clay watched helplessly as the guy moved back toward the doorway, pulling Jesse with him. He couldn't allow him to leave with her. He'd have to wait until the guy went outside, though, before he could tackle him.

If he went out through the French door and around the house, he could surprise him out front. He knew he could count on the others to grab Jesse and keep her safe.

As soon as the crazed man moved to the doorway, Clay saw Jake make his move. Jake grabbed the arm holding the knife, forcing it away from Jesse.

Clay grabbed Jesse by the arm, flung her in Blade's direction and leapt at the intruder. The knife flew out of the man's hand and Clay did what he'd wanted to do since seeing a knife at Jesse's throat.

He smashed his fist into the bastard's face with the force of a brick, knocking the man out cold.

He looked over the fallen man to Jake who he'd inadvertently knocked down.

"Sorry, Jake. You okay?" Clay stood, looking down at the unconscious man on the floor.

"Yeah," Jake stood and grinned at his friend. "She's going to give you as much trouble as her sister gives me."

"God help us." Clay knew that Nat provoked Jake at every opportunity and that Jake had to constantly be on his toes to keep up with her.

Clay also knew how Jake loved it.

Clay turned to see Jesse being crushed to Rio's chest. They'd both been hurt and would have to be taken to the hospital.

He strode across the room to the two most important people in his life.

Watching Jesse fuss over Rio's injury, he hugged her from behind.

"You okay, baby?"

He took the damp towel Blade used to wipe the blood from Jesse's neck.

"It looks like it's okay." Lifting her chin, Blade eyed her neck critically. "It needs an antibiotic ointment and should be bandaged."

Rio moved closer to see for himself. Ethan stood next to him and nodded in agreement.

"Yeah, something like that could get infected. You'll have to keep changing the bandage. Keep it dry."

"I can't believe this!" Jesse cried incredulously. "Rio's been shot and you guys are worried about this little scratch."

Rio frowned at her. "It's just my arm, Jesse. That guy almost slit your throat."

Jesse blinked in surprise and looked at each of the men in turn. They all wore worried frowns as they stared back at her.

Jesse shook her head. Nothing in her life had prepared her for men like these.

She turned to Clay. "We need to get Rio to the hospital."

"We'll get both of you to the hospital, baby, as soon as Ace gets here."

Jesse touched Rio's arm below the makeshift bandage. "Does it hurt a lot?"

Rio leered at her. "Later you can kiss it and make it better."

Tears filled her eyes. She could see the pain he tried to hide.

"He could have killed you," she choked.

"He could have killed *you*." Rio eyed her darkly. "Don't think you won't be spanked for disobeying me and leaving the locked bathroom."

"And for taunting a man holding a knife to your throat," Clay added menacingly.

Blade and Ethan nodded in agreement, obviously happy to add their opinions.

"She has to learn to obey you," from Blade.

"Jesse's going to have to learn to trust you to keep her safe. She's going to have to learn to remember that. A red bottom would remind her," Ethan added.

Jesse looked over to where Jake stood guard over the fallen man to see him watching her. She winked at him and turned back to her men.

"I was so scared," she whispered, pouting. "I didn't think. I'm so sorry."

She sniffed. "I was so afraid you got hurt. I heard the shot and I just wanted to get to you. I want both of you to be my husbands. I love you so much."

She pushed her bottom lip out and saw the tenderness in her men's eyes. Maybe she wouldn't be getting that spanking after all.

Jesse and the others turned when Ace walked into the room, taking in the scene at a glance.

"Who knocked this guy out?" He gestured to the man on the floor.

"Clay," Jake said. "One punch."

Jesse watched as Ace moved into the room, his eyes taking in the damage. His brow lifted when he saw the knife, then the gun.

"How bad are you hurt?" The towel on Rio's arm had become soaked with blood.

"I'm fine," Rio dismissed with a shrug. "The bastard cut Jesse, though. We need to get her to the hospital."

They heard a moan and looked over to see the man getting shakily to his feet. His expression looked desperate when he saw that three large men surrounded him, making escape impossible.

Jesse shook off the hands holding her and raced toward him. That bastard had broken into their home and shot Rio.

When he tried to raise his arm, Jake grabbed it.

Blade halted her with an arm around her waist.

"Easy, tiger."

"You shot Rio, you jerk." She struggled against Blade's grip.

Jesse continued to struggle even though Blade had lifted her off the floor in his attempt to hold her. She continued to rage at the man who'd shot Rio, threatening various parts of his body with her wrath.

"Jesse!"

Jesse froze at Clay's shout.

He moved beside her as Blade cautiously lowered her feet to the floor.

"That's enough. Let's get you and Rio to the hospital."

Jesse looked up at Clay and nodded. Blade released her and before anyone could stop her, she spun, kicking the intruder in the groin and watching as he folded.

"Damn it, Jesse."

Chapter 17

Clay looked up from the steaks on the grill. Filled with satisfaction, he studied the scene before him.

It was the night before their wedding and Jesse wanted to spend the night at the new house with her sister doing whatever women do when they're alone.

Thank God Jesse had finally calmed down.

All of their sons had come for the wedding, his, Rio's, Jesse's and Jake and Nat's boy.

Jesse had fretted Will and Kyle wouldn't like her and had grilled him and his brother relentlessly about what they liked and didn't and about their favorite foods. She and Nat had then spent several days getting both houses ready, shopping for and cooking enough food to feed a small army.

Clay smiled. These four ate like an army.

By the time they'd all arrived, Jesse had been a nervous wreck. Both he and his brother had tried unsuccessfully to reassure her.

She hadn't calmed down until both Will and Kyle had a private conversation with her. He hadn't had a chance to ask them yet about it, but he would.

Meanwhile, Will, Kyle and Alex had spent the last several days sleeping in this house, their days spent getting to know each other and their soon-to-be step-parents. This house had more bedrooms and would be kept ready for whenever the boys wanted to use it.

Clay and Rio planned to sleep here tonight after the women insisted that they couldn't see Jesse again until the wedding.

They took this as a great opportunity to spend man-only time with the boys. They'd asked Jake and his son Joe to join them, thinking that Alex might be more comfortable having his uncle and cousin there.

Both Will and Kyle seemed to be taken with Jesse, Clay thought to himself, immensely pleased.

He and Rio had seen Alex's confusion and worry at first at the thought that two men would be sharing his mother. They'd understood his concerns and answered his questions patiently. Joe had taken Alex to town and introduced him around, making a special point to introduce Alex to Gracie and her husbands and Isabel and her three doting husbands. They knew Alex had talked to his uncle, too, and had gradually warmed to them.

But, today Alex seemed awfully quiet as they all gathered on the patio. Something bothered Alex and Clay wanted to get to the bottom of it. Nothing would be allowed to interfere with their wedding to Jesse, but Clay wanted everything settled so nothing would mar her day.

Jesse would be frantic if her beloved son seemed unhappy.

He glanced again at Alex. The boy smiled at his cousins and soon-to-be step-brothers' antics but the smile didn't reach his eyes. He hid a lot, the way his mother had.

He and Rio had already decided to pay for Alex's college and had their argument to Jesse prepared. They would be Alex's stepfathers. Alex's own father remained in jail. If she wanted them to be a family, they would do for Alex what they did for Will and Kyle.

Alex deserved no less.

He saw Rio flick a worried glance at the boy and nodded in understanding when Rio looked at him. Jake intercepted their look and shook his head warningly.

Clay bit back his impatience. Apparently Alex had confided in Jake. For whatever reason, Jake wanted them to let it go for now.

When they'd finished eating and had the mess cleared away, the boys talked the men into playing poker with them, insisting that poker should be included in 'man's night'.

Besides, they'd argued, they wanted to work on their game and thought it would be fun to beat the 'old guys'.

"Old guys?" Rio growled, causing the boys to laugh hysterically at his outraged expression.

"You think that's funny, do you? Well us 'old guys' are gonna clean you young pups out of all your matchsticks. Let's see who's laughing then."

Playing with them proved to be completely different from their games at the club. None of the boys had a poker face worth a damn and they showed each other their cards, asking for advice on what to play.

Clay, Rio and Jake tried to hide their amused grins, enjoying the game more than they had any other.

Over two hours into the game, the boys' piles of matchsticks had steadily dwindled. They each contemplated the hands they'd just been dealt in silence.

"I'd like to say something."

Clay lifted his eyes to see Alex regarding both he and Rio intently. His stomach clenched. He glanced at his brother. Rio looked just as nervous.

"What's on your mind, Alex?" Clay forced himself to keep his tone light.

He watched Alex shift in his seat and glance at his uncle. At Jake's encouraging nod, he began.

"When mom told me she wanted to get married again, I got scared. I was partly scared for her, I mean, she and my dad didn't seem happy together. They weren't even really together all that much."

He snuck glances at them while he appeared to study his cards.

Clay would bet his prized stallion that Alex couldn't name a single card in his hand.

"I also got scared for me," Alex continued. "What if her new husband didn't want me around?"

"I hope you know how welcome you, all of you, are here." Clay's look included his son and nephew. "The new house has only one bedroom but this house has plenty of room and will be kept ready for the three of you whenever you want to use it. You can visit or you can live here. It's up to you."

Clay watched the boys look at each other. Something passed between them, but they looked back at their cards when Alex cleared his throat.

"When I heard my mom wanted to marry two men I got really scared." Clay's heart broke when Alex lowered his head and murmured softly. "I think my dad would have hit my mom before if I hadn't been there. He didn't want to look bad in front of me. I didn't even want to go away to school, but mom said to do what I needed to do. She told me she would be divorcing him."

"Are you afraid we would ever hurt your mother?" Clay asked carefully, silencing Rio's automatic protest with a raised finger.

"I was," Alex confided. "Until I talked to Uncle Jake and I saw the way you are with her."

Now Clay's heart melted when Alex's voice broke. He could see the boy's struggle for control, clearly not wanting to cry in front of them, but needing to finish.

"I've never seen my mom happy, really happy, until now." He turned pain-filled eyes to him and Rio. "I didn't even realize how unhappy she was before." He cleared his throat again. "Thanks for making my mom happy."

Clay's tight stomach relaxed and he smiled at Alex.

"Your mother makes us just as happy."

Clay frowned when Will and Kyle laughed.

"What's so funny?" he asked, surprised and furious that they would laugh at Alex.

Will sputtered. "That's what we said to Jesse."

Kyle reached over and slapped Alex playfully on the shoulder.

"When we talked to your mom yesterday, we said to her what you just said to Uncle Clay."

Will smirked at Alex.

"Yeah, when we said it though, you're mom cried, but," he added mischievously, "we got brownies!"

* * * *

Jesse stood between her husbands wearing only the silk teddy she'd worn under her wedding gown.

Their eyes had blazed when they'd first seen her in the peach silk she'd worn to be married in.

Their eyes darkened now as they paused in the process of undressing her to circle around her, the looks in their eyes making her blood start to heat.

Jesse felt cherished. Neither of them had been more than a few feet from her all day and made no pretense of being happy that she'd married them.

She'd hoped they'd like her teddy but had underestimated just how much. They just stood and stared at her, lust and love warring in their eyes.

She knew the white satin and fine lace teddy molded her figure to perfection. It pushed her breasts high and molded her bottom in a way she hoped enticed them. Peach ribbons trimmed with more of the fine lace tied into bows and strategically placed held the teddy in place.

Ribbons tied over her breasts served as straps. Several tiny ribbons tied into bows held the sides together and three more over her mound held the teddy in place between her legs.

She'd had it specially made by the talented woman who owned the lingerie shop in town who'd been ecstatic over Jesse's design and wanted to make more for her store. She'd promised more to Jesse in an array of colors at cost in gratitude.

This one she'd paid plenty for and seeing the looks on Clay and Rio's faces, she knew it had been worth every penny.

"Oh, God, baby."

Clay's hand actually trembled when he reached out to trace one of the ribbons over her breast. It looked even smaller and more fragile under his large hand.

Rio, who had stood staring for several long moments, finally spoke.

"Darlin', you are so beautiful." He looked at Clay, and Jesse smiled at the deep contentment in his eyes. "She's finally our wife."

Clay nodded, his eyes still on Jesse. "Worth every bit of the wait."

Rio took a step back and circled her again, his grin making her shiver in excitement. Clay's intense stare glittered with promise and she found her knees becoming weak.

Rio chuckled. "So all that stands between us and getting you naked are these tiny little ribbons." He traced a finger over the small bow tied over her other breast.

When Jesse nodded, smiling coyly, Clay leaned in, his lips feather light as he nibbled at her lips.

"I have never seen anything so incredibly sexy in my life. Thank you, baby."

"All of your clothing should be like this." Rio slowly pulled the end of the ribbon, teasing them all, until the bow came untied, both Clay and Rio watching, mesmerized.

One by one they untied each bow with excruciating slowness, Clay and Rio taking turns, their hands and mouths exploring every inch of exposed flesh, until finally she stood nude between them.

Jesse trembled and fought to breathe. They seduced her so slowly and thoroughly, their touches light and fleeting, she squirmed helplessly, desperate for more.

They'd both looked so devastating in the suits they'd worn but she knew they looked even more devastating with them off. Their jackets and ties had come off before they got home. Their shoes and socks had come off at some point until they wore just their dress shirts and slacks.

Amidst long drugging kisses and frustratingly teasing touches, she'd managed to strip their shirts from them. Running her hands and lips over their sleek muscles, Jesse marveled that they now belonged to her. She flicked their male nipples with her tongue, power surging through her at their responses.

She lightly bit into Clay's muscular chest as she slowly unbuttoned his slacks. Her fingers found the tab on his zipper, lowering it slowly, skimming her hand lightly over his rock hard length.

Clay's breath caught when she got to her knees and lowered his slacks and boxers.

Jesse placed open mouth kisses on his thighs, slowly working her way up toward his impressive cock, the head large and red and pulsing with need.

A drop of pre come glistened on the tip. When Jesse touched her tongue to lick it off, Clay jerked and hissed, grabbing her shoulders and holding her away from him.

"I'm too aroused, baby. I won't last. Rio and I want to both be inside you when we come, when we take you for the first time as your husbands."

Jesse looked up at him from beneath lowered lashes.

"You'll have to exercise that control you're so proud of. You and Rio have been teasing me. It's my wedding night, too. I want to taste my husbands' cocks. Would you deny me?"

"Damn it, Jesse." Rio chuckled at Clay's groan and watched his brother squeeze his eyes shut. Rio looked down and his own cock jumped when he saw his adored wife on her knees, her mouth inches from his brother's cock. He almost exploded on the spot.

"Just a little?" Jesse pleaded.

Clay released her shoulders and Rio watched his brother battle for control.

Rio knelt behind Jesse, chuckling as he reached for her breasts.

"Surely you can hold on for a few minutes, Clay. If our wife wants a cock in her mouth, we should oblige her."

His cock jumped again when Jesse reached up and caressed his jaw and whispered. "Don't laugh, stud. You're next."

While Jesse worked on his brother's cock, Rio worked on her, vowing to put an end to his bride's smug teasing. He wanted to make her so hot that she forgot all about teasing them and begged to be taken.

He pulled and plucked at her nipples in the way he knew drove her wild. He looked over her shoulder, loving the sight of his hands on her.

He heard his brother's moans and smiled as he pinched Jesse's nipples hard enough to have her moaning, too.

"Not so smug now, are you, darlin'? Let's see if I can do better."

He released her breasts and reached for the lube. Squeezing a liberal amount onto his fingers, he looked up to see Clay watching him. "Let's make her beg."

"Fuck!" Clay groaned and closed his eyes again and Rio knew Jesse had stepped up her game. Well he could do that, too.

Wrapping an arm around her waist, he touched his fingers to her tight opening and felt her jolt.

"You know what comin', don't you, darlin'?"

He pushed two fingers inside her tight bottom and felt her clench on them.

"You are so tight, darlin'." He continued to stroke her, pushing further with each thrust and could feel the way her body trembled. He loved those little mewing sounds she made in her throat.

"Darlin', I can't wait to shove my cock up your ass. Let's see how smug you are then."

He knew how wild she got when they talked to her like this and by the way she trembled harder, knew his rough talk had turned her on even more.

"I'm going to take you so slowly that the burn you love so much is gonna last a long time. You're gonna be stretched so tight that I'll have to hold still so I don't come right away. But that's not gonna happen until I'm all the way in, darlin', so far in that it'll feel like I'm in your throat."

Rio heard Clay groan and saw him push against Jesse's shoulder, jerking his cock from her mouth.

When Jesse reached back for him, he eased his fingers from her ass and moved to stand in front of her, sharing a look with Clay.

He knew his brother would take over and drive Jesse wild. He took a deep breath, bracing himself for the first touch of her hot little mouth on his cock. Christ, he hoped he could last. His cock was already hard enough to pound nails and he didn't know how much of fucking his wife's mouth he could take.

Rio smiled when he saw that her hands shook when she reached for him. He watched as his brother moved in behind her and lay on the floor, lifting Jesse up and over him until she sat on his face.

He smiled at her startled look. "Not so confident, now, are you, darlin'?"

He saw the determination on her face before opening her mouth and leaning close and he braced himself.

The feel of her hot mouth on his cock had him hissing. Oh God. She turned him inside out.

He gripped her head in his hands and began stroking her mouth as she used her diabolical little tongue on him. The slurping noises she made just made him hotter, as did the tortured moans coming from deep in her throat.

Feeling the vibration of her moans on his cock, he knew he wouldn't last.

Her nails dug into his thighs and he knew Clay's mouth had zeroed in on its target. A fine sheen of perspiration covered her and she began sucking him more desperately into her mouth.

Suddenly he couldn't stand another second and jerked out of her mouth, watching as Clay caught her.

Thank God Clay grabbed her, Rio thought as he gripped the footboard of the bed tightly and struggled for control. His knees felt weak and he knew that if not for his tight grip on the wood, he would have fallen.

"Damn, Jesse," he groaned. "That mouth of yours is lethal."

Rio looked over, mesmerized by the sight of Jesse on her knees over Clay's face. Clay had his hands on her hips. Jesse had a tight grip on his forearms, her knuckles white.

Her head was thrown back in abandon, her entire body flushed with pleasure. Her cries and moans sounded more desperate by the second. He knew her now, knew what those sounds meant.

Rio had regained enough control to move back to her, holding her tightly as she trembled, his mouth covered, swallowing her moans.

One hand covered her breast, tweaking at her nipple while the other moved to the cheeks of her bottom, sliding his fingers down the crease until he touched her lubed anus.

Rio worked two wide fingers into her bottom, stroking deeply as he continued his assault on her breasts, moving from one to the other, pinching her sensitive nipples hard enough to make her jolt.

He used his mouth on hers, loving the sounds coming from deep in her throat. He knew that Clay had moved from under her and had moved in behind her and felt his brother's hands brush his chest as he covered Jesse's breasts.

The time for play had ended. He wanted his cock in her. Now.

He pulled his mouth from hers and lifted her slight weight in his arms and looked over to see the strain on Clay's face as he lay back on the bed and held out his arms for Jesse.

Rio handed her off to his brother and watched as Clay pulled Jesse over his chest and tilted her head for his kiss.

Rio braced a hand on her back and used the other to grip his throbbing cock and poise it as her lubed hole. Watching the head disappear into his wife's ass almost had him coming on the spot.

Jesse tore her mouth from Clay's and made that gasping sound that fired his blood and jerked but he used his hand on her back to keep her in position.

He began thrusting inside her, gritting his teeth as she clenched on him.

"You have the most incredible ass." Rio groaned harshly as he painstakingly gave her his entire length.

When he had finally seated himself to the hilt inside her, he pulled her gently off Clay's chest and back against his, his arm wrapped around her waist. Nuzzling her neck, he breathed in her scent.

God he'd never get enough of her.

"I love you, Jesse." He nipped at her earlobe. "I love being inside you. It doesn't matter if I'm in your wicked mouth, your sweet pussy, or your tight ass. When I'm inside you, I'm in heaven."

It was the most romantically erotic thing he'd ever said to her and it brought tears to her eyes even as it sent a spark of new awareness through her.

She watched Clay's face as he parted her folds and nudged the head of his cock to her pussy opening.

"I love you, baby." Clay's eyes gleamed, holding her enthralled. "Open for me, baby." He pushed into her slowly, driving her insane until he filled her completely, both holding themselves still, deep inside her.

"Your husbands love to fill you, wife." Rio's harsh groan in her ear made her shiver.

Jesse could feel every bump in their cocks as she stretched around them.

"Oh, God, I love you both so much."

He body clenched and spasmed around their throbbing cocks. If they didn't move soon, she didn't think she'd survive. Her body stretched with an erotic pain that continually surprised her with the devastating effect on her senses.

She simply lost herself in the demands her body made and forced those demands on her new husbands to satisfy.

"Move," she demanded. "It's too much. It's not enough."

Her hands fisted on Clay's chest, her eyes closed as she arched.

"Please. I need you," she begged.

"With pleasure," Clay growled.

"There's nothing I like more," Rio growled.

After so much foreplay, their lovemaking became almost violent in its intensity.

Jesse knew from experience just how strong her orgasm would be and couldn't help but struggle against its magnitude.

Jesse felt Rio thrust forcefully into her bottom and heard his harsh grown as he came, pulsing deep inside her. Oh God. What those pulses did to her. She couldn't prevent clenching on him. She felt so full.

They filled her. They surrounded her. They made her burn.

With Rio holding her tightly from behind, Jesse felt anchored and with no defense left, she burst deep inside, sparks shooting through her body like electric charges. She screamed hoarsely, her voice nearly gone as her body tightened almost painfully.

She heard Clay's deep groan and felt his hands tighten on her hips as he came long and hard.

No one moved as they all struggled to recover, heavy breathing and moans the only sounds in the room.

After several long minutes, with a soft kiss to her shoulder, Rio lowered her to Clay's chest, and he immediately wrapped his arms around her. Rio withdrew from her slowly, forcing another moan from her. He patted her bottom softly before moving away.

She knew he'd gone to get a warm washcloth to take care of her as they always did. She hadn't become entirely comfortable with it yet, but they'd both insisted on the ritual and she found herself getting used to it.

She knew she glowed with happiness. The love and attention they heaped on her made her delirious with a joy so deep it scared her. She'd actually woken in the middle of the night more than once, fearing it had all been a dream.

Each time, both Clay and Rio reached out to soothe her, somehow always tuned to her even in sleep.

Cuddled between her husbands, she lay spent, engulfed in warmth. Drowsy with satisfaction, she leaned back against Clay, idly stroking Rio's arm. The bullet wound had almost healed and would leave a scar. She cringed with remembered fear every time she saw it.

"I can't believe we're married," she breathed.

She stopped her stroking to raise her hand, admiring the two new bands she wore, one on each side of the twin diamonds they'd given her.

Clay lay facing Jesse, smiling indulgently as he watched their wife looking at the rings they'd placed on her finger only hours earlier

"I have two husbands," she said softly to herself.

"Yes, we know, darlin'," Rio teased.

She poked his chest in retaliation, giggling when he flinched.

"Careful with those nails, darlin'. I already have imprints of them on my butt."

"I have them on my arms this time," Clay chuckled. "She really digs in when she gets excited, doesn't she?"

He rolled to his back, sated and happier than he'd ever been. He closed his eyes and felt Jesse shift next to him.

"We shouldn't have sex anymore."

"What?" Clay heard Rio's incredulous yelp and felt the bed shift.

"Like hell," Clay growled without opening his eyes.

"Well if you can't handle my nails digging into you when I come, maybe it would be better if we don't have sex, I mean, if you're too delicate…"

Clay chuckled at her taunt and looked over as Rio rolled on top of Jesse, smiling at his brother's outraged expression.

"Delicate? Can't handle you? I can handle anything you dish out, wife."

Clay turned back to his side facing them and stroked Jesse's soft shoulder as Rio covered her mouth with his. When Rio lifted his head, he couldn't help but chuckle at Rio's disbelieving expression as he looked at Jesse.

"Delicate? You think I'm delicate?"

Clay heard Jesse giggle and looked over as she slapped a hand on her mouth, her eyes twinkling.

"Minx," Rio muttered with a self depreciating grin.

"She's gonna be trouble." Clay snuggled her back against him and reached over to turn off the light.

"We're gonna have our hands full," Rio agreed.

"I have two husbands to keep up with," Jesse reminded them. "I have two very possessive, overprotective, sometimes outrageously frustrating husbands to deal with every day. But if one of you gets angry with me, you can always pass me off to the other."

"Never!"

Clay reached over to flick the light back on, turning her to face him, his eyes sharp.

"You belong to both of us at all times, Jesse. You're *our* wife, baby. Believe me, you're going to be able to handle us. We're the ones that have to keep up with you." He stroked her face lovingly and smiled as he touched his lips to hers. "I look forward to every day now. Having you as our wife has made us happier than either of us has ever been."

He watched Rio stroke her bottom and shifted to turn off the light. "And if you start causing us trouble, we'll just have to remind you who's boss." He grinned at his brother's threat as he lay back and settled Jesse against him.

Jesse sighed. "Training both of you is going to take a lot of work."

Silence filled the room.

"Excuse me?" Clay lifted his head to search her features in the dark.

"Sshhh, I'm sleepy," she answered drowsily.

After a while Rio muttered across Jesse's sleeping form. "Train us? What the hell did she mean by that?"

"I don't know," Clay answered softly so as not to wake their sleeping wife. He smiled in the darkness. "But it's gonna be a lot of fun finding out."

Epilogue

One week later Jesse watched in amazement as the huge amount of pancakes she'd prepared disappeared with alarming speed.

She had a hard time just keeping up with her husbands' appetites. Adding their sons and hers to the mix and the amount of food they went through staggered her.

Glancing over, she watched Clay's strong teeth bite down into a strip of bacon. Her lips curved, remembering what those teeth had been doing a short time ago and how she'd satisfied another of her husbands' big appetites.

She saw Rio's eyes narrow as she looked at him and winked, smiling coyly at him as she bit into her toast. She watched his eyes go to her lips as she ran her tongue over them and smiled mischievously. When he glared at her and shifted in his seat, she lowered her eyes and struggled to keep from laughing out loud.

"Why are you smiling like that, baby?"

Jesse looked up at Clay's question, meeting his eyes over the rim of her coffee cup. She saw the boys glance up at her curiously, distracted by food, but Clay's gaze sharpened.

"I've been watching all of you eat and thinking about what big appetites you have."

The boys laughed at her observation, flexing their muscles, trying to outdo each other.

But her husbands knew her well. The knowledge of what she'd been thinking shone in their eyes.

When they both shifted in their seats, their eyes blazing, she knew they remembered their early morning loving.

With a smirk at their predicament, Jesse rose to clear the table.

"Mom, wait."

Jesse sat, turning a questioning look at Alex.

"What is it, honey?"

Her stomach dropped to her toes when she saw the way he and the other two boys looked at each other.

Oh, God. They were leaving.

She loved having them all here. She'd just started to develop a relationship with Kyle and Will as Clay and Rio developed one with Alex. She saw a huge difference in her son. He'd become more confident and playful under Clay and Rio's guidance and attention. She knew they spent a lot of time talking to Alex and that he went to them sometimes for advice.

Brian had never been around much and Jake had tried, but being so far away, he couldn't give Alex the attention he'd needed.

"The three of us want to talk to all of you about something."

No. Please don't let them say they're leaving. She wanted more time with them.

Jesse turned her eyes to Clay, then Rio. She felt her icy hands engulfed in Clay's warm one.

Facing the boys, she tried desperately not to cry.

"If it's alright," Will began, "we'd like to spend the summer here."

Jesse looked from one to the other, afraid she'd misunderstood.

"If it's okay," Kyle added with a glance at the others, "we talked about transferring to the college close to here. We could start in the fall."

Alex added, his voice brimming with excitement, "If we shared an apartment, we could stay there during the week, come here on weekends and breaks."

Will looked at Clay. "Dad, we thought about spending this summer doing some work on the house."

Kyle turned to Rio. "If we find jobs in town, we could use the money for paint and stuff. The furniture's pretty old but we can save to buy some new stuff."

Clay raised his brow at his son. "Have you talked to your mother about this?"

"No," Will admitted. "She's busy with her new family and I hardly see her when I go there. Besides, I never get to see Kyle anymore."

"Yeah," Kyle added. "Will and I always wanted to be brothers like you and Uncle Clay. Now we have Alex."

"Now the three of us can be brothers." Will punched Alex's arm playfully.

Jesse's eyes filled with tears at the look on her son's face.

When she spared a glance at her husbands, she could see they appeared just as moved.

She couldn't take it in. She burst into tears and ran from the room, too overcome to speak. She heard the scrape of chairs and low voices as she ran down the hall and into the bedroom.

She dropped to the edge of the bed and buried her face in her hands and struggled to get her tears under control. The bed dipped and she felt herself being lifted onto Clay's lap.

"I can't believe they're staying." She sobbed softly. "I thought they were going to tell us they were leaving."

"I take it you're happy about them staying." Rio smiled wryly.

Clay kissed her hair, his hands gently running up and down her back and arm as he spoke to his brother.

"Rio, what if we give them the money, a budget for them to use to fix up the house the way they want. It'll give them something to do all summer and they'll get to know each other better, working together on a project like that."

"I think it's a great idea." Rio nodded as he knelt in front of her, taking her hands in his.

"We haven't done anything to that house in so long because we were busy building this house, waiting for Jesse to show up." He grinned at her disarmingly. "That house needs a lot of work. We'll tell them we're available when they need help but won't interfere. Well, not too much anyway."

Jesse felt Clay's arms tighten around her. "I don't want them working on the electrical and I certainly don't want a basketball court in the living room." He turned Jesse's face to his. "What do you think, baby? If the boys work on the house together and fix it up the way they want, it'll feel like their home."

"Well, darlin', what do you think?"

Jesse looked at each of her husbands in turn and smiled through her tears.

"I think," her voice broke, "I think I married the most incredible men and that I'm the luckiest woman in the world."

Clay lifted her face and used his thumb to wipe a stray tear from her cheek. He pressed his lips to hers. They felt warm and firm and sent her heart racing. When he eased back, his eyes blazed with emotion.

"We're the lucky ones, baby. Our lives were empty before you came into them."

"You're our world, darlin'." Rio pulled her close to kiss her tenderly and her heart leapt. "Because of you, we have our sons and yours here with us. A real family. We'll take care of Alex the way we take care of Will and Kyle. We're all family now, Jesse, because of you."

Clay kissed her forehead. "And you are the center of it."

"Come on. Let's go tell the boys our plan. They've had enough time to clear the table," Rio teased.

Jesse walked back into the kitchen with Clay and Rio trailing behind her. The boys turned at their entrance, their faces hopeful. Jesse felt the tears running down her face as she hugged each of them in turn.

They would be living right next door!

She could never have imagined ever being this happy. She looked over to see her husbands smiling at her indulgently, their own eyes moist.

She'd taken a chance on a life she'd never imagined and found happiness and love she'd never known.

Moving to her husbands, she listened to the boys make plans, closing her eyes as Clay and Rio moved close, surrounding her once again with their warmth and knew she'd never be cold again.

DESIRE FOR THREE

Desire, Oklahoma 1

THE END

ABOUT THE AUTHOR

Leah Brooke has always loved to read and has always been addicted to happily ever after. After reading one of her mother's romance novels, she was hooked. Being somewhat of a daydreamer, plots for stories and reading stories made her wonder, "What if?"

Finally she started to put them on paper. It took years of working on stories for her own amusement before a manuscript was born and she decided to send it in.

She's been married to her high school sweetheart for more than twenty years and has two sons whom she describes as being the light of her life, and who contribute greatly in helping her keep her sense of humor.

Siren Publishing, Inc.
www.SirenPublishing.com

SIREN PUBLISHING

Leah Brooke

Desire, Oklahoma 2

BLADE'S
DESIRE

Siren Publishing

Ménage Amour

Leah Brooke

Desire, Oklahoma 3

CREATION OF
DESIRE

Printed in the United States
213253BV00004B/94/P